Filthy Cowboy

Filthy, Volume 5

Amy Brent

Published by Amy Brent, 2021.

This is a work of fiction. Similarities to real people, places, or events are entirely coincidental.

FILTHY COWBOY

First edition. March 1, 2021.

Copyright © 2021 Amy Brent.

ISBN: 979-8201066208

Written by Amy Brent.

Also by Amy Brent

Filthy
Filthy Boss
Filthy Doctor
Filthy Professor
Filthy Seal
Filthy Cowboy
Filthy Daddy
Filthy Coach

Forbidded
The Doctor's Fake Marriage

Forbidden
Fake Fiance
One More Chance
Crave Me
My Best Friend's Dad
The Doctor's Fake Marriage
Dad's Best Friend

Forbidden Fantasies
Daddy's Business Partner
Daddy's Friend
Daddy O
Climbing His Corporate Ladder
Taken By Daddy's Boss
Filthy Liar

Standalone
Teachers' Pet
Filthy Box Set
Knocked Up By My Brother's Best Friend
My Best Friend's Brother
My Best Friend's Ex
Say You're Mine
Club Desire Box Set
My Boyfriend's Dad
Fighting For Her
Forbidden Love Box Set
Love Undercover
Friends With Benefits
A Royal Menage
Baby Fever
Vegas Baby
Brother's Best Friend for Christmas
Christmas With My Best Friend's Dad
My Son's Sitter
Single Dad's Christmas Present
Surrendering To 3 Alphas

Because I Love You
Catching Up With Daddy
Claiming Cinderella
Double Trouble
First Love
First Time
Knocked Up By My Brother's Best Friend
My Best Friend's Boyfriend
Pretend Daddy
Redemption
Roomies With Benefits
Royally Yours
Rub Me The Right Way
Show Stopper
That One Night
The Baby Contract
Truth Or Dare
Santa's Naughty List
Quickie on Christmas
Con Man

Table of Contents

FILTHY COWBOY

by
Amy Brent

This is a work of fiction. While, as in all fiction, the literary perceptions and insights are based on life experiences and conclusions drawn from research, all names, characters, places and specific instances are products of the author's imagination and used fictitiously. No actual reference to any real person, living or dead, is intended or inferred.

I swear, Luke Daniels is as stubborn as a mule and hung like a horse. He spends his time drinking whiskey, riding bulls, and sleeping with every horny woman in west Texas. I gave him my virginity and my heart when I was just a girl. Now, it's payback time...

I haven't seen Luke in six years. He was my first lover, my first love, and the first boy to break my heart. But he had his dreams and I had mine, so I was fine with never ever seeing him again.

Okay, that's a lie. I've missed him every day – and every night – for six years. I long to have him back in my life. And back in my bed. And back between my legs.

Then he's almost killed by a bull and I'm sent to bring him home. The old spark instantly ignites. All I can think about is riding him like a bucking bronco, like I used to, even though he's stitched up like a baseball and not supposed to do anything strenuous.

The question is, now that we're back together, will Luke come to his senses and stay with me? Or will the lure of the rodeo once again tear him from my arms?

Luke Daniels

Here's a tip for you fellas out there the next time you're laid up in the hospital after a goddamn bull gores the living shit out of you at a rodeo.

Hell, I guess this is a good tip regardless of why you're laid up.

Anyway.

If you ever get the chance to fuck a hot young nurse in your hospital room bathroom, I highly recommend you take it. Just grab that bull by the horns and ride her like there's no tomorrow.

That hot young nurse had been giving me warm-lotion hand jobs for three days, ever since they took the catheter out of my pecker so I could piss on my own. Shit, she'd had my pecker in her hand more than I'd had it in mine.

Started out, she was just gonna help me into the bathroom to take a piss. I wasn't wearing anything but one of those flimsy hospital gowns, which she untied and tugged down my arms after coming into the bathroom with me and closing the door. I stood there naked as the day I was born, with my long pecker dangling between my legs for the whole world to see.

Without a word, she reached down and cupped my balls with her left hand and started tugging on my pecker with her right. The damn thing went hard in her hand so fast it made her moan.

She let go of my pecker, then pushed down her scrub pants to her ankles and leaned over the sink and stuck out her ass and said, "Fuck me hard with that big old thing, cowboy. Fuck me hard right now."

Never let it be said that Luke Daniels didn't follow a medical professional's advice. I dug my fingers into her hips and squared up behind her, then drove my big old pecker into her tight little twat like pushing a sausage through a straw. Hot damn, this little girl was tight, man. Tightest little pussy I'd ever seen. Course, any pussy's gonna be tight when you stick something in it as big as my pecker. Still, I looked down to make sure I'd stuck it in the right hole.

That little nurse grunted every time I thrust it into her, like it was pushing all the wind out of her lungs. I put my hands on her chubby little ass cheeks and watched my pecker slide in and out of her. I could only get about half of my pecker inside her, but it felt like heaven on a stick. My balls were tight as walnuts and I could feel the blood pumping in my loins.

There is no better medicine, in my opinion, regardless of what ails a man, than a piece of sweet, young, tight pussy. I love the way it feels, the way it looks, the way it smells, and the way it tastes.

I'm telling you, fellas, if they could bottle this little gal's pussy the world would be a healthier place. And you and me would be addicted with the first dose.

As I hammered into her, listening to her gasp and moan, I thought about what sweet, caring individuals nurses were, especially the ones who had to put up with the likes of me. I was a lousy fucking patient, no pun intended. If that goddamn bull's horn hadn't ruptured my appendix and spleen, I would have just put a Band-Aid over the gash and gone on about my day.

Not that I had any say in the matter when it happened.

As I understand it, I was laying there in the goddamn dirt with my guts spilling out all over my sterling silver National Rodeo Champion belt buckle and the fucking rodeo clowns were all puking their guts out around me. If there hadn't been a veterinarian there wrapping a horse's leg I would have probably bled to death right there in the Houston arena, like goddamn Spartacus or something.

Fucking rodeo clowns. Goddamn pussies, every single one of them.

Anyway, like I was saying, nurses are such caring, sweet individuals who go above and beyond to take care of their patients. God bless their souls and God bless this little girl riding my pecker who was now making sounds like her top was about to blow.

She was bent over the sink with her cheek pressed to the mirror, holding onto the sides of the sink for dear life, saying she was about ready to cum. I was right there with her, buddy. The moment she slid home I was coming in right behind her.

I suddenly learned that not all nurses are that dedicated to the health and rehabilitation of their patients. The one that jerked open the bathroom door and started screaming when she caught me slamming my sausage into the young nurse's twat did not see the humor of the situation.

She was a fat old hag with a butch haircut and a face that could stop a clock. She stood there in the doorway, getting all red-faced and fuming like she'd caught us fucking in the back of the church or something.

I gave her an "I'll be with you in a minute" smile, but didn't stop what I was doing. I just kept hammering it to the young nurse while she stayed bent over, grabbing the sink and grunting each time my big old cock slammed into her tight box.

I could see sweet thing's face in the mirror. She didn't acknowledge the nurse standing in the doorway watching us. She just kept her eyes closed and her mouth hanging open. I reckon she figured she was screwed anyway (again, no pun intended), so she might as well hang in there long enough to get her rocks off rather than stop midstream. Or mid-stroke...

"What the hell do you think you're doing?" the old nurse wailed after she had watched us for ten of fifteen seconds. I reckon it took her that long to comprehend that she wasn't imagining things.

"I'm just doing my physical therapy," I said, my hands tight on the girl's hips to hold her steady while I rammed it to her good. I shook my head and grinned at the old bat without missing a beat. "I had no idea how much better this would make me feel. You ought'a give this little gal a raise. She's a goddamn miracle worker."

"Stop that before you bust your stitches!" she yelled, waving her hands at me.

"Darlin', I'm not gonna stop till I bust this nut," I yelled back, ignoring the pain that was ripping through my left side where the bull had gutted me. His fucking horn stabbed into my guts about six inches they said, then he picked me up like a rag doll and shook his big old head, twisting my guts around like a meat grinder before tossing me to the side.

The doc had patched up my guts and sewn up the gash about a week ago, so I was still healing. There was a big bandage on my left side covering the wound, with a mile of gauze wrapped around my waist to keep it in place.

I also had several cracked ribs and they were taped up, but they didn't bother me much. I'd cracked my ribs so often I felt funny if I didn't have a pain when I breathed.

Even though it hurt like a motherfucker and I could look down to see blood soaking into the bandage, I wasn't gonna stop poking it to this little gal until I blew my load in her hot box. I expected the old nurse would understand and be okay with it after she had time to think things over. Every man feels better after bustin' a nut.

And brother, I was getting close and I was feeling fine.

The young nurse moaned and pushed her ass back against me. My big old pecker just kept ramrodding her like a derrick drilling for oil. She said she was cumming, so I quit holding back and came right along with her.

I was glad we were about done. The old nurse standing in the door watching us was starting to give me the creeps.

I closed my eyes and gritted my teeth and came like a bursting dam. I gave her a few more good thrusts just to make sure she got hers, then collapsed back on the toilet seat.

My big old cock slid out of her and flopped wet and nasty against my leg.

My side hurt like a son of a bitch.

The patch covering the wound was now drenched with blood. Blood was seeping from under the bandage, sluicing down my left hip and leg like a little stream running south.

The last thing I remembered before blacking out was the old nurse yelling at the young one, the young one tugging up her pants and crying, and thinking that I had died just like I wanted to; while fucking a sweet young piece of pussy that milked my old pecker like a milking machine.

And if that had been the last thought to go through my head, that would have been just fine with me.

Luke

I woke up back in the hospital bed where I'd been lying for the last week. The doctor was there, a humorless little fucker with thick glasses and cold hands named Shively. He was shining a fucking bright light in my eyes and asking if I knew my name.

"My name is get that fucking light out of my eyes," I said, trying to wave him away with a hand that wasn't quite working right. I heard him say something to the old nurse who had walked in on me boning the young thing. She was on the other side of the bed, changing the dressing over the gash in my side. Obviously, the woman had no comprehension of the concept of being gentle. She was poking and prodding me with the finesse of a goddamn one-armed butcher.

"You can't get out of bed without assistance, Mr. Daniels," the doctor said, sliding the pin light into the front pocket of his white lab coat. He leaned over my belly and poked his fingers around the wound. Lightning bolts of pain shot through me and almost made me jump off the bed.

"Fuck, man," I said, leaning my head up to glare at him. "Get your fucking fingers out of there."

"You busted your stitches," the nurse growled as she finished redressing the wound. She had one of those deep husky man voices like she'd been smoking cigarettes and drinking rotgut whiskey all her life.

I made the mistake of glancing into her eyes. She was still pissed at me, but I thought I saw something else there, maybe a little spark of lust, given that she did help get me back into bed with my sticky pecker hanging out. It probably just took one good look at it to melt all the rust off her old cooch.

Jesus, I hoped she didn't come back later wanting to ride my knobby pony. She was a big old girl with dark hair on her upper lip. If she climbed on top of me it'd probably kill me. Then again, I've stuck my cock into bigger, uglier women, but that was always late at night after getting a snoot full of booze. Funny, how your standards drop the later at night it gets.

I'll be honest with you, fellas. I've woken up with some coyote ugly women in my days. I call them coyote ugly because I was like a coyote with its leg caught in a trap. A coyote will gnaw off its own leg to get out of a trap. If a coyote ugly woman was laying on my arm, I would have gnawed it off to get the fuck away from her.

"Can you give us a few minutes, nurse," the doctor said, nodding toward the door. The nurse huffed at me and gathered up the stained bandages and carried them out the door.

The doctor stuck his pudgy fingers under his glasses and rubbed his eyes. He blew out a long sigh and shook his head at me. "Mr. Daniels, I'm going to tell you once more. You cannot get out of that bed without someone helping you."

"I had help getting up," I said, smiling through the pain. "And I had help getting off."

He cleared his throat and shook his head again. "You do realize that you probably cost that girl her job."

I winced as I brought my hands up behind my head. "Oh come on, doc. They ain't gonna fire that girl just because we were having a little game of hide the sausage in the bathroom."

"You're wrong," he said. He took off the glasses and cleaned them on his tie. "Nurse Pritchett is on her way to human resources right now to file a complaint. At the very least, the girl will be suspended for a week or two without pay. At worst, she will be fired without references." He set the glasses on his nose and glared at me through them. "So, I hope you're happy with yourself. I hope it was worth it."

I grinned at him. "Jesus, doc, did you see that little girl? Big old tits, big old ass, pussy tighter than Dick's hatband. Of course, it was worth it."

He lifted his chin and looked down his nose at me. "You really are an asshole, Mr. Daniels."

I held out my hands and smiled. "Guilty as charged, doc," I said. "Guilty as charged. Now, cut the shit and tell me when I can get the fuck out of this place. I'm starting to get bed sores lying here."

"You had massive internal injuries where that bull gored you," the doctor said. "And you just busted your stitches. You're not going anywhere for at least another week."

I pushed myself up on my elbows to shoot him a hard look. It hurt like a sumbitch, but I wasn't gonna let him know it. "Doc, you either sign my fucking release papers or I'll walk out of here on my own."

He folded his arms across his chest and huffed at me. "You wouldn't make it half a block before you collapsed and bled to death."

I nodded at the window. "I'd rather die on the sidewalk out there than die in this bed in here." I locked onto his eyes so he would know that I was not fucking around. "I can't spend another week in this bed. I'm not cut out to be a fucking patient. I make my living on the backs of bulls and broncos. Every minute I lay here I can feel my body dying. I need out of here, doc. I need out of here now."

He blew out a long breath and held out his hands. "Fine, I can release you in two days if you have someone who can at least look after you for a week or two, just in case you do something stupid and bust those stitches again." He wiggled a finger at me. "Seriously, Mr. Daniels, if you bust those stitches again you could get a serious infection or even bleed to death."

"I'll be careful, doc," I said, falling back on the pillow. "My pal Cody said I could stay at his place until I was all mended up."

"Okay, then I'll release you in two days." He had my chart under his arm. He flipped it open and scribbled something on a page.

"Fine," I said, closing my eyes. Without warning, a sharp pain shot up my left side and crashed into my brain. Fireworks started going off in front of my eyes. I felt a cold sweat wash across my face. My stomach started churning like a cement mixer. For a moment, I thought I was going to hurl chunks in the air.

The doc glanced at me from over the chart. He saw the color draining from my face and the sweat dotting my forehead. He gave me a smug look but didn't move to help. He tapped the medical chart on the foot of the bed. "See, this is what I was talking about. You need to stay here."

"Fuck you," I said, gritting my teeth at him. "I'm getting out of here in two days, with or without your approval."

"Okay, Mr. Daniels," he said, moving toward the door. "It's your funeral."

"Fucking A right it is." I managed to stay awake long enough for him to leave the room, then my head started to swim and I passed out dead to the world.

Shelby Cates

"I refuse to have that boy in this house!" I said it like I owned the place and slammed my fist down on the table to make my point. The silverware jumped and Daddy's cup of hot coffee almost sloshed over. "He ain't nothing but trouble and I will not have him here."

"Settle down, Shelby," Daddy said slowly, waving his fork at me as if it were a magic wand that could put his only daughter in her place. He blew out a long sigh that made the long whiskers in his mustache bristle.

"First off, he ain't a boy, he's a man, and second, this ain't your house. Least not yet. When I'm gone, it'll be yours and your brother's to fight over. Till then, I have the say on who can sleep under this roof and who can't."

I sat on the edge of my chair at the other end of the table fuming at him. I just couldn't believe Daddy would allow such a low-life piece of crap like Luke Daniels to stay under his roof.

In the meantime, my idiot brother, Cody, who brought up the topic of bringing his best friend, Luke, to the ranch to recover from getting gored by a rodeo bull, sat between us silently picking at his breakfast like a man keeping his head down hoping to go unnoticed during a bar fight.

"Luke's always been like family, Shelby, and you know it," Daddy said, stabbing another sausage link with his fork and bringing it to his plate. "Now granted, sometimes he's been the black sheep of the family, but we don't turn our backs on family, regardless of color."

"What the hell does that even mean?" I snapped.

"It means you need to hush up and let me eat my breakfast in peace. I swear, you're getting to be just like your mother." He cut the link in two with the side of the fork and stuck half in his mouth. When he chewed, his mustache wiggled. When I was a little girl I thought it was cute. Now it just annoyed the heck out of me.

Daddy wiggled the fork at me again. "I swear, that woman could give me heartburn before breakfast just by looking at me. Don't you try to do the same."

"You gonna run Shelby off, too, Daddy?" Cody asked, grinning, cutting his eyes at Daddy. He was referring to the day fifteen years ago when Mama came home to find her bags packed and sitting outside the front gates of the ranch with Daddy standing there with his shotgun cradled in his arm. He had found out Mama was sleeping with a cowboy in town and that was all she wrote. Me and Cody stood inside the gate watching with tears in our eyes.

Mama didn't bother to deny it or place blame. She'd been caught fair and square, and she knew Daddy was not a man prone to forgiveness after he'd been cheated on. I admired Daddy's restraint. He just told her to pick up her bags and git. When he was a younger man he would have tracked her and the cowboy down and gutted them both like a deer.

"You hush, too," Daddy snapped at Cody, though he was trying not to grin beneath the mustache that covered his lips.

"But Daddy, Luke Daniels ain't nothing but trouble," I said again, sitting back and crossing my arms over my breasts. I was starting to feel like a lousy lawyer arguing a losing case. My only argument against Luke Daniels was that he was "nothing but trouble" because that's all I could say about him without riling Daddy up to the point of violence.

There were lots more things I could say about Luke, but I never would, not to Daddy, the man who still treated me like I was his virginal little girl. In his mind, I was still as chaste as mountain snow. He'd shit in his hat if he knew how many boys I had slept with in high school and while I was away at college. His little girl was no slut, but she hadn't been a virgin since the day she turned sixteen. Luke Daniels saw to that.

I hadn't seen Luke since the day I left for college six years ago, but I expected that he hadn't changed much. Too good-looking for his own good, more muscles than brains, didn't give a rat's patoot about anything or anybody other than riding bulls and having a good time. And by good time I meant that he would drink anything you put in front of him and screw anything that moved and some things that didn't. Cody always said Luke was stubborn as a mule and hung like a horse. I knew from personal experience that points were true.

Fuckin' hell... it annoyed me to no end that the mention of Luke Daniels' name could make my nipples hard. My waterworks were going, too, like somebody had turned on the faucet down there. I could feel hot moisture pooling in the cotton panties between my legs. Try as I might, it seemed I only despised Luke from the neck up, because from the neck down, it was party time.

"Why do you hate Luke so much, Shelby?" Cody asked, giving me a sideways glance. He picked up another biscuit and swirled it around the gravy left on his plate. He popped the entire biscuit into his mouth and chewed slowly while giving me a knowing smile.

"I just do," I said, growling at him. "That boy's been nothing but trouble since the day he was born." Daddy was watching us from the other end from beneath his bushy eyebrows.

"You keep saying that Luke ain't nothing but trouble," Cody said, glancing at Daddy but talking to me. "What'd Luke ever do to you to make you hate him so much?"

"He never did anything to me," I snapped. "Just shut up and eat your damn biscuit."

Anyone listening would have thought that we were little kids the way we argued, even though I was twenty-six and just home with a master's degree in agriculture from Texas A&M, and Cody was a twenty-eight-year-old cowboy who helped daddy run the ranch.

I glared at Cody. He knew why I hated Luke Daniels, and he knew better than to say anything in front of Daddy. Daddy might have shot Luke with both barrels of his old shotgun if he knew what happened between us. Cody knew that, too, which was why he would never say anything.

Cody just rolled his dark eyes and shook his head. Cody looked more like Mama than Daddy. He had jet black hair that hung in his steel blue eyes and sharp Cherokee features. He was big and tall and rugged and had never started a fight, but was always ready to finish one if somebody was picking on me or Luke. His skin was the color of dark honey, year-round.

I looked more like daddy; tall and thin, with strawberry-blond hair that I kept pulled back into a long ponytail at the base of my neck, blue eyes, and fair Irish complexion that refused to tan even in the hot Texas sun. I had to wear long sleeves and a floppy hat to keep from burning when I went outside.

Crazy that I had gotten a Masters in agriculture, I know. I planned to spend more time doing seed research in nice, air-conditioned labs than tromping around outside in the scorching Texas sun.

Cody was easygoing like Mama and I was a stick of dynamite ready to explode like Daddy was at my age. Time had mellowed him. I couldn't imagine it doing the same to me.

Cody and Luke had been like brothers since the day Luke's parents were killed in a car wreck out on Highway 9. Luke was two months younger than Cody, so Cody always treated him like a little brother.

Luke's daddy was my Daddy's best friend and lead ranch hand. Luke came to live with us when he was twelve and I was ten. We all grew up together, but Cody and Luke were thick as thieves. You never saw one without the other.

Luke never gave me a second glance until I started filling out my t-shirts and bikini tops, then, like most girls in Calloway County, it became my life's mission to get Luke Daniels to notice me... to touch me.

He always called me "Lil Sis" up until the day I left for college. The only time he didn't call me Little Sis was when he was taking my virginity in the barn on my sixteenth birthday.

Sometimes I wondered if Cody was really all right with what happened between me and Luke all those years ago. He had always been a protective big brother to us both, but when it came to Luke, he always seemed ready to give him a pass.

It made me sad sometimes that Cody hadn't beaten the shit out Luke when he caught us in the barn that night, his best friend and his little sister fucking like rabbits in the hayloft. Cody hadn't said a word. He just blinked at us for a moment, like he couldn't believe his eyes, then went back down the ladder out of sight so me and Luke could finish what we were doing.

I guess Cody understood that Luke wasn't forcing me to do anything I didn't want to do, since I was the one on top, riding Luke like a rodeo cowgirl trotting around the arena on her prized stallion.

I was the one who had dragged Luke out to the barn while everyone else was enjoying my Sweet Sixteen birthday cake.

I was the one who begged Luke to pop my cherry.

I was the one who wanted him to be my first.

At the time, I wanted him to be my first, last, and only.

Maybe I still wanted that.

Maybe that was the problem.

Maybe that was why I was so damned afraid of seeing him again.

Luke

"I still think you should wait a few more days," the doctor said, giving a disapproving shake of his head as he read over my chart for hopefully the last time. "You pop those stitches again and – "

"I know, doc," I said, holding up my hands. "I could bleed out and die."

He shot me a hard look over the top of his reading glasses. "Yes, without immediate medical attention, you could bleed out and die."

"I understand, doc," I said. "Don't you worry. I plan to outlive you by a good thirty years just so I can say I told you so."

I offered up the best smile I could muster. My side still hurt like a sumbitch, despite the pain meds and antibiotics they'd been pumping into me for over a week. It felt like somebody was sticking a hot branding iron into my gut, but I wasn't gonna let him know that. I held up my right hand and said, "I promise to be careful. Scouts honor."

"I seriously doubt you were ever a Scout," he mumbled. He held out his hands and sighed like a man who was giving up. "All right then, you have been warned and I bear no responsibility for anything that happens to you once you walk out that door."

"Agreed," I said. "I am on my own. Got it."

He closed my chart and tucked it under his arm. He took off the glasses and tucked them into the front pocket of his white coat. He asked, "Do you want me to prescribe pain meds to go with the antibiotics?"

"Don't need pain meds, doc," I lied. "I just need some clothes and directions to the elevator."

I was sitting on the edge of the bed with my feet dangling, still wearing a flimsy hospital gown and nothing else. I'd been told that my bloody clothes had been cut off me by the EMTs and thrown away. The only things that survived were my bloodstained National Rodeo Association Championship belt and silver buckle (they knew I'd skin them alive if they hurt that belt) and my scuffed boots, which were sitting on the floor next to the bed with the belt tucked inside one of them. Far as I knew my old truck, along with everything I owned like clothes and a wallet that didn't have more than a few dollars in it, was still sitting in the parking lot at the rodeo arena.

Sweet Thing—the cute little nurse that I'd banged in the bathroom a couple of days before—came in carrying a pair of blue hospital scrubs for me to go home in. The doctor watched her like a hawk as she set the scrubs on the bed next to me and quickly left the room without ever looking me in the eye. Too bad. I would have loved to have tapped that sweet ass one more time before being released. Oh well. Maybe I'd look her up the next time the rodeo was in Houston.

I had convinced the old bat of a nurse not to report Sweet Thing for what we'd done. It was all my fault, I said. Don't punish her because I can't keep my pecker from getting hard. Don't ask me how I convinced her because that is a tale I will not tell. Let's just say that sometimes a man must do things he wouldn't otherwise do sober and leave it at that.

"Do you need help with that?" the doc asked, watching me struggle with the scrub shirt. I got my head in okay, but when I raised my arms it felt like somebody was sticking a chainsaw in my guts. I grunted at him as I got the shirt over my arms. He stepped in to tug the shirt down carefully over my bandaged side. My face was washed with sweat and I felt like I was gonna puke, but I held up a hand to shoo him away.

"I'm okay," I said, my voice a hoarse whisper. I closed my eyes and breathed deeply for a moment. Slowly, the nausea subsided. I picked up the scrub pants and slid them up my legs and cinched them at my waist. Without underwear to keep it in place, my junk kind of bulged out the front of the thin scrub pants. Oh well. Nothing I could do but let it hang.

I tossed the hospital gown on the bed and pulled the belt out of the boots to set it on the nightstand. I ignored the dried blood that coated the silver buckle and dark leather. I didn't have any socks, so I just slid my bare feet into the boots.

It took all the energy I had just to get dressed. I leaned back on the pillows and closed my eyes. Cody would be here soon to take me home where I could rest without a bunch of doctors and nurses fussing over me. I swear, these people would wake you up to give you a sleeping pill.

"Okay, Mr. Daniels," the doc said with a tone of finality, still shaking his head at me. "I've done all I can do. I'll go sign your release forms and the nurse will be in shortly with a wheelchair to roll you downstairs."

He put a hand on the pointed toe of my boot and gave it a little wiggle. "Behave yourself, Mr. Daniels. I don't ever want to see you in here again."

"Don't worry, doc," I said quietly. "Next time a bull gores me in the gut I'll make sure they just let me die in the dirt."

Shelby

I just about had a hissy fit when Daddy told me that I would have to drive four hours to Houston to pick up Luke from the hospital because he and Cody were going to be busy nutting young bulls all day.

Actually, I think the correct term is "de-nutting".

If you don't know what that means, look it up for yourself because it's too disgusting for me to talk about.

Anyway, when Daddy told me that Luke would be released later in the day and I had to pick him up, I said no fucking way. Let him take a bus or a taxi. I wasn't going to spend four hours getting there and four hours back, stuck in a truck with Luke Daniels.

No way.

Forget it.

Shit.

Needless to say, I was still fuming when I pulled into the Houston Memorial Hospital parking lot and went to the desk to ask what room Luke Daniels was in. I was directed to take the elevator to the fifth floor, room 518. I got in the elevator and when the doors slid shut, I checked my reflection in the mirrored surface.

I was wearing skin tight jeans with the legs tucked into a pair of old cowboy boots, and a denim shirt rolled up to the elbows and tied at the waist, over a white camisole that showed off a fair amount of my freckled cleavage.

I had my hair pulled back like always and had even put on a little makeup. Silly, I know, but I wanted Luke to look at me and see what he missed out on when he left all those years ago.

Look at what you could have been fucking all that time, I wanted to say.

Look at what you could have had riding you like a buckin' bronco.

Then again, by now we probably would have been divorced and fighting over custody of a couple of rugrat kids.

I don't want them, you take them.

No way, they're yours...

By the time the elevator dinged and opened to the fifth floor, I had just about decided that maybe it was best that Luke had left me behind.

If he hadn't left home to ride the rodeo circuit, we might have gotten married and I might never have gone off to college to get my degrees and create a life of my own.

I might have lived my whole life on a dusty Texas ranch popping out babies and washing dirty diapers and wiping snotty noses while wondering if their daddy was ever gonna come home.

Maybe he did me a favor by leaving me behind.

Maybe I'm the hard-headed, strong-willed woman that I am today because Luke Daniels took off one day and never came back.

Maybe I was better off.

I guessed I'd never know.

* * *

Luke was in room 518. I held my breath as I walked down the long hallway, counting room numbers as I went. 510... 511... 512...

When I reached room 518, I paused for a moment to peek through the open doorway. It had been six years since I'd seen Luke. I was eighteen and he was twenty. We'd had sex dozens of times. We'd kept our relationship (if you could call it that) secret because Luke didn't think Daddy would approve and he was probably right.

We weren't exclusive or anything. I dated other boys and lord knows he went with other girls. But we had a bond that kept bringing us back together. Or at least I thought we did.

Then one day Luke said he was hitting the rodeo circuit and didn't know when he'd be back. I was stupid in love with him and he was stupid in love with the rodeo. He just drove away and left me standing there in the dust waving goodbye like the village idiot. I kept waiting for him to turn around, but he never did.

Peering through the door, I held my breath, wondering how much he had changed, if he had changed at all.

The last time I saw him he was a strapping young bull rider with broad shoulders and a thick chest, and arms that were roped with muscle from hanging on to the backs of thousand pound bulls.

He had shaggy blond hair that hung down in his blue eyes and a smile that made me melt in my panties. His skin was the color of tanned boot leather from a life spent in the Texas sun.

He looked like a young Brad Pitt and he knew it.

And he took advantage of it every chance he got.

Besides me, he probably screwed half the girls in Calloway County and would have screwed the other half if he'd had the time.

All he cared about was getting drunk, getting laid, and hanging on to a bull for eight seconds to get a silver buckle.

I knew it at the time and I knew it now, Luke wasn't the kind of boy you expected to stick around. He was like an angry Brahma bull: you might get a rope around his horns, but there was no way you were gonna tie him down.

The man lying in the bed in room 518 vaguely reminded me of the boy I'd once known, but as we say here in Texas, he looked like he'd been rode hard and put up wet.

He was lying on his back with his eyes closed and his hands resting over his stomach. He looked a little ridiculous, wearing a pair of blue hospital scrubs tucked into a pair of dusty old cowboy boots.

His complexion was pale, sickly, like he'd been out of the sun for a while. His sandy blond hair was pushed back and plastered to his head, like it hadn't been washed in days. His chin and cheeks were hollow and stubbly.

I hadn't seen him in six years, but he looked like he'd aged a couple of decades.

I took a deep breath and let it out slowly, then stepped forward and tapped on the door. When his blue eyes opened and he smiled, the past came rushing back like a tsunami crashing into the shore.

My old Luke was there within that shell of a man.

I knew it because I felt my body tingle the moment I saw him smile.

Luke

I was lying there with my eyes closed, breathing slowly in and out, trying to will away the burning pain in my side, when I felt like I was being watched.

I opened my eyes just enough to see someone standing in the hallway outside my door. I couldn't tell who it was exactly or whether she was there to see me or someone else.

It wasn't until she knocked on the door and stepped closer that I realized who it was. I felt my heart jump into my throat. It was Shelby, Lil Sis, come to take me home.

"I'll be damned," I said, smiling when her face came into focus. "What are you doing here?" I held out my arms to hug her, but she just reached for my hands and gave them a loose shake.

"Cody sent me to pick you up," she said flatly, giving me a smile that I could tell was forced. I tried to remember if I'd done anything to make her mad, as was the case with most women in my past. Honestly, I couldn't even remember the last time I'd seen her, or if we had parted in good company. Too many concussions will do that to you, I guess.

"He too busy to come get me himself?" I asked, grinning, hoping she would grin back. She did not. She just shrugged her pretty eyebrows at me and said she reckoned so.

Time had been extra good to Shelby. She looked amazing in her tight jeans and little white shirt with her cleavage bubbling out. Her face was flawless except for the freckles that dotted her nose and cheeks. I used to count them with kisses after we made love in the barn loft. She was always the prettiest girl in Calloway County and that had not changed. She didn't look like an awkward teenager anymore. She looked like a woman; so much so it made my mouth water. I couldn't help but wonder what it would be like to make love to her now.

"So, are you ready to go?" she asked, getting right to the point. Yep, I had done something to her and she was still stewing over it. I just wished that I could remember what that something was.

"The nurse will come with a wheelchair when I buzz her," I said, wincing as I pushed myself up on the bed. My side bit at me when I tried to sit up. I put a hand over the bandage and pushed through the pain as I pressed the button to call the nurse with my other hand.

Shelby sat in the chair next to the bed, giving me the suspicious eye, like she thought getting gored by a damned old bull shouldn't have put me in such a sorry state. She asked, "So what happened?"

I lifted my shirt so she could see the bandage and the wrapping going around my waist. "Oh, I just pissed off a bull is all," I said, my fingers gently going over the tape holding the bandage in place. "He decided to show me some love by sticking his horn in my guts and tossing me around a little. Ain't no big deal."

"Do not listen to him," a voice called from the doorway. It was Nurse Old Bat pushing a wheelchair into the room. She gave Shelby the once over for a moment. "You his wife? Girlfriend?"

Shelby frowned back at her like she'd been accused of farting in church. "No, I'm... family," she said, though she didn't sound too proud of the fact. "I'm here to take him home."

The nurse narrowed her eyes at Shelby like she was trying to figure out if she was telling the truth or not. I would have loved to tell you that Nurse Old Bat looked much nicer when she was at the peak of orgasm at the end of my fingers, but that would have been a lie. That was her face, for better or worse. After a moment, her harsh features softened a little and she nodded at me.

"You sure you want to leave?" she asked, sounding a little like she didn't want me to go. "The doc's not happy about this."

"The doc just wants to pad his bill," I said, giving her a smile. I nodded at Shelby. "I'll be in good hands."

"I'm not going to be your nurse," Shelby shot back. Her words slapped my face like a horse's tail swatting a fly. She frowned at Nurse Old Bat. "Tell me the extent of his injuries and what needs to be done. I'm sure my Daddy will hire a nurse to look after him."

Nurse Old Bat leaned on the wheelchair and let her eyes go between us. It was easy to tell that one of us was pissed at the other, and the other had no idea why.

She said, "When he was gored by the bull there was extensive damage done to his stomach and spleen, which had to be removed. The doctors were able to repair the damage and stitch him up, however..." She shook her head at me. "Mr. Daniels managed to rip his stitches open a few days ago and that had to be repaired, so he's still healing."

"How did he rip his stitches open?" Shelby asked. When Nurse Old Bat looked at me, so did Shelby. "How did you rip the stitches open?"

"He tried to go to the bathroom by himself," the nurse answered for me. "He got dizzy and fell and busted the stitches."

Shelby's pretty face took on a mask of concern that had not been there before. "Is that still a possibility? Him passing out when he tries to go to the bathroom?"

Nurse Old Bat shook her head. "It wasn't that he was using the bathroom, dear," she said, glancing at me again. "It was the fact that he was doing something he wasn't supposed to be doing. He wasn't supposed to get out of bed without help. He has a hard head, this one."

Shelby nodded slowly. I could tell by her face that she knew she wasn't getting the full story. She said, "I'll make sure he has someone to help him until he's strong enough to get around by himself."

"I don't need a goddamn babysitter," I said, feeling a little bit like a fly on the wall with them talking about me like I wasn't even there. "I just got dizzy is all. I'm fine now."

"Are there any medications that he needs?" Shelby asked, ignoring me. "Prescriptions to be filled?"

"He'll be on antibiotics for another week," Nurse Old Bat said. "He has refused painkillers."

Shelby frowned at me. I could almost detect a hint of giving a shit in her pretty eyes. "Why don't you want pain killers?" she asked.

I set my jaw and shook my head. "I've seen a lot of cowboys get hooked on pain killers," I said. "I won't go down that road." I tried smiling at her again, still with no effect. "Besides, they'd interfere with my whiskey drinking."

"You're hopeless," Nurse Old Bat said, a rare smile on her face. She nodded at Shelby. "He just needs lots of bed rest. And don't let him do anything strenuous that puts pressure on his stitches."

"I understand," Shelby said.

I couldn't resist giving the nurse a wink. "Can you define strenuous?"

"You know exactly what I'm talking about," she said, smiling at me. She wasn't half bad looking when she smiled. She was probably a looker twenty or thirty years ago. She nodded down at the wheelchair.

"Okay, cowboy, come on, I have real patients to tend to. Climb on and let's get you out of here before you get somebody else in trouble."

Shelby

I got the strange feeling that there was something going on between Luke and the nurse that they didn't want me to know about. And there was more to the story than she was willing to tell about him busting his stitches.

I stared at her while she was talking to him. Her eyes kind of went dreamy when she looked at him and Luke blushed like a boy who'd been boning his teacher after class. I would not have been surprised in the least if you had told me Luke had laid pipe to half the nurses in the place, but to this one? No freakin' way.

Her name tag just read: Dottie. She was thick and dumpy, probably in her mid to late forties, with chopped off reddish hair and a face that I doubted put too many patients at ease. Surely Luke had not done anything with this one. I mean, no offense, but... ewe.

Dottie helped Luke get into the wheelchair. There was a thick leather belt with a large silver buckle on the night stand. He asked me to hand it to him.

When I picked it up I noticed the dark brown stain of old blood on the buckle and the belt. I felt my stomach churn. That was Luke's blood all over that old belt. I glanced at his face. He was still kidding around with the nurse, but I could tell that he was in pain. He was hurt far worse that he was letting on. Cody said that he almost died. I didn't believe it at first. I figured it was just Luke looking for attention. But I had been wrong. He was seriously hurt.

"Hey." I heard Luke's voice and the sound of fingers snapping.

I blinked a couple times. Luke was holding out his hand and wiggling his fingers. "Hand over my championship belt, Lil Sis," he said with a smile. I felt like I was in shock as I handed him the belt and followed them out of the room.

* * *

I went to get Cody's truck while the nurse wheeled Luke to the sidewalk to wait for me. As I pulled to the curb, I saw several other nurses gathered around his chair telling him goodbye; younger, hotter ones, all smiles and hugs.

The older nurse shooed them away and helped Luke get to his feet and into the truck. She leaned in to buckle his seatbelt, then gave him a kiss on the cheek and told him to take care of himself.

"What was that all about?" I asked, frowning at him as he waved her away. "Please tell me that you didn't – "

"Jesus, Shelby, she's a nurse," Luke said, shooting me a scolding look. "It's her job to be nice to sick people. Maybe you should try it sometimes."

"If you say so," I said, giving him the once over before putting the truck into gear. "You all set? Need anything?"

"I just need to get the hell away from this place," he said with a sigh. He leaned his head back on closed his eyes. "Goddamn hospital was gonna be the death of me."

It occurred to me that he was leaving the hospital with nothing more than the borrowed clothes on his back. I asked, "Where's all your stuff?"

"In my truck at the rodeo arena," he said, his voice strained. He wiped sweat from his forehead on the back of his hand. I could tell he was in pain, though I knew he wouldn't admit it. "I'm not too worried about it. There ain't much there to steal. Let's just go home. I'll worry about it later."

"Okay," I said, sliding the gear into Drive and pulling slowly out of the lot. "Sit back and relax. We'll be home in four or five hours."

We were barely a mile down the road when I heard him begin to snore. I glanced over at him. His head was back on the headrest, his eyes were closed. He was breathing softly through his cracked lips. His left arm was resting on the console between us. I resisted the urge to touch his hand.

I was glad he had fallen asleep. I still wasn't sure what to say to him. Maybe this would give me a little more time to figure it out.

Shelby

We'd only been on the road for an hour or so before it started getting dark. The highway going north out of Houston toward Calloway County was an old four-lane with no street lights and very few places to stop. I'd gassed up the truck before I picked Luke up, but my stomach was starting to growl at me. I decided I'd stop at the next burger joint or convenience store we came to so we could get us something to eat. We were still a good three or four hours from home.

Luke was still passed out dead to the world in the passenger seat. He smacked his lips and mumbled a few times, making me glance over at him. When I looked at him I still saw the handsome boy I grew up with. The boy I had willingly given myself to. The boy I thought I loved. The boy who still haunts my dreams.

I noticed he slept with a hand covering the wound on his left side. Every now and then he'd wince and jerk in the seat. He tried to make light of it, but I knew his wound was serious. The bull that had gored him, a sixteen-hundred-pound monster named El Diablo, had killed another rider the year before. Luke was lucky to be alive. And even though I was still pissed at him, I felt lucky to at least have him back in my life for however long I could convince him to stay.

The hypnotic drone of the tires on pavement and Luke's soft snoring were making me sleepy. I turned on the radio just loud enough to hear it. I searched through the dial until I heard an old familiar song: *Wonderful Tonight* by Eric Clapton. It was playing the last night I was with Luke. It had always reminded me of him. And it always would.

* * *

I was just eighteen the last time I saw Luke, but I thought I was ready to take on the world. I had spent my entire life on a dusty Texas cattle ranch and now it was time to spread my wings and fly out into the great big world to see what my future might bring.

Luke was feeling the same, although our paths would take us in completely different directions.

He was just twenty and so full of life people would have paid to be around him. All the boys wanted to be him and all the girls wanted to fuck him. He was always happy and smiling and carrying on some kind of mess, but he was never happier than when he was hanging onto the back of a mad bull or a bucking bronco.

I loved watching him back then, the way the muscles in his right arm flexed as he held on to the latigo, hoping to hang on for eight seconds, the minimum time required to earn points.

He'd dig in the heels of his dirty boots into the side of the bull and let his left arm flail in the air as his whole body came up off the bull's back and slammed back down. He always lost his hat right out of the gate. His long blond hair whipped as the bull's hooves beat into the ground and it bucked its curved back, doing its best to throw him off.

All Luke could talk about was getting on the circuit so he could travel from town to town riding bulls and collecting trophies and silver belt buckles. His ambition only went as far as the next town and the next bull. That was one thing we argued about sometimes. I was hell bent on making something of myself and Luke has hell-bent on being the next Ty Murray.

Even though we knew we'd be apart for some time, I thought we had an understanding that one day we'd meet back in Calloway and start a life together. I reckon it's like my daddy always said: you can plan out your life, but eventually life will get in the way of your plans.

The last time we made love was in the early fall when the air in Texas gets just slightly less humid and the days don't last as long. I had already enrolled in Texas A&M and was set to leave at the end of the week for College Station. Luke had entered a rodeo in Brownsville and was set to leave first thing in the morning. This was not supposed to be our last night together. It was just supposed to be our last night together for a while.

Luke had an old pickup truck that was held together by rust and duct tape. We used to sneak off it in and drive out to Myers Lake and park on the river back and make love in the bench seat. Or it the back. Or in it lake. Or on the hood. Heck, we were like horny little rabbits back then. We'd do it anywhere, anytime, any way we could.

Luke pulled up to the end of the lake and put the truck in park. He set the parking brake because the old truck had a tendency to roll. He shut off the clunky engine, but left the radio on. Wonderful Tonight came on and Luke started singing to me. The boy had lots of talents, but singing wasn't one of them. I told him to quit singing and kiss me.

It was after nine o'clock, but the full moon shining on the lake gave the cab of the truck a warm, bluish glow. We had the windows down. A cool breeze was wafting in. It made my nipples stand on end as Luke pulled my t-shirt over my head. I wasn't wearing a bra. I never wore a bra when I was with Luke. It only slowed him down.

I shimmied out of my cutoff jeans and panties while he stripped off his clothes. I leaned back against the door and brought my legs up in the seat. Luke moved in on me with a grin on his face. He pressed his moist lips to mine as his hands kneaded my tits. He rolled my nipples between his fingers. I moaned and sucked on his tongue. I could feel my hot juices pooling in my young cunt, sluicing down my taint and asshole, filling the truck with the scent of my sex.

I reached for Luke's cock, finding it hard and ready, like always. The boy was hung like a horse and it took two hands to hold it all. I slowly worked my hands back and forth, sliding the skin over the hard muscle. I cupped his balls. They were tight and warm. I gently rolled the sack between my fingers as my other hand milked his long cock.

"I want your cock inside me," I sighed in his ear. My tongue slid inside his ear. He giggled and pulled back so he could look at me. His left hand remained on my breast as his right hand slid down my stomach toward my pussy. I didn't trim my pubes back then, so I had a pretty good crop of strawberry-blond curls. Luke playfully scratched at the hair for a moment, then slid his long finger over my clit and into my pussy, finding me soaking and hot for him.

I closed my eyes and put replaced his hands on my tits with my own. I squeezed my milky globes until it hurt. My nipples were long and thick. I took them between my thumbs and forefingers and gave them a squeeze.

Luke pushed himself up and took his cock in his right hand and stroked it as he watched me play with my tits. Our eyes met and he smiled. I was too young to know what love was back then, but I was sure he loved me just by the way he looked at me.

"You want some of this?" Luke asked, squeezing his cock to make the head mushroom. A little drop of juice came out of the slit. I wiped it off with the tip of my finger, then put the finger in my mouth.

"Yes," I moaned, pushing my hips off the seat. "I want your big cock inside me. Now."

"Yes, ma'am," Luke said with a grin. He gripped my hips and pulled me toward him. He pressed the bulbous head of his cock to my hole and slid it around for a moment, lubing it up. I was young and tight and he we big and girthy. We had to be careful because his cock could have literally ripped me in two.

The breath caught in my throat when he slid in the head. I felt my pussy opening for him, spreading, waiting to take him inside. I put my hands on his arms and held my breath as he slid in another inch, and then another. When he got half way in, he hit my cervix. It always made him smile when that happened. He began to slowly draw his cock out, then slide it slowly back in.

My body caught fire as my pussy stretched and squeezed his massive cock. He closed his eyes and moaned. "Goddamn girl, that has to be the tightest pussy in Texas."

"You complaining?" I asked, giving him a sly smile.

"No, ma'am," he said, the words coming on gusts of breath. "I'm just happy to be invited to the party."

"Then shut up and fuck me, cowboy," I said, hands squeezing my tits again.

Luke started hammering it to me, pushing me against the door with each thrust. I swear, that old truck felt like it was rocking back and forth. He thrust into me as far as he could do, then quickly pulled back and thrust in again. I could feel his cock filling up my entire body. I could feel him in my chest and in my head. I imagined that I taste his cum in the back of my throat.

"Fuck... Luke... fuck... yes... oh shit... yes..."

"I'm cummin," he moaned, his body tensing up. I opened my eyes to watch him. Every muscle along his shoulders and neck were thick and pumped, with veins pulsing the blood toward his cock. He closed his eyes and gritted his teeth. He was cumming, long and hard, filling me with hot seed. I could feel it pumping into me, hot, thick, wonderful.

I curled my toes and came with him. The orgasm hit with a shudder that made my whole body jump. My pussy ignited, sending shockwaves to every nerve. I squirted my juices all over his cock, all the way back to his dark pubes and balls.

He thrust into me a few more times, then blew out a long sigh that seemed to deflate his entire body. With his fingers still dug into my hips and his cock still inside me, Luke gave me a sad smile and shook his head.

"I'm gonna miss you, Lil Sis," he said.

I smiled back at him with tears in my eyes. "I'm gonna miss you, too."

The next morning I stood in the front yard with Cody and Daddy, watching Luke drive away in his old truck. I waved along with them with tears in my eyes.

I had no idea at that moment that it would be six years before I saw Luke again. If I had known, maybe I would not have let him drive away on his own.

Shelby

"Hey, Shelby, did you hear me?"

I thought I was still lost in my memories when I heard Luke call my name. I shook my head to clear it, then glanced over at him. "I'm sorry. What?"

"I asked where we were?" he said, sliding up in the seat. He held on to his side and winced as he looked out the windows. "Damn, it's dark already."

"It's been dark for a while," I said. "We're still a couple of hours out. There was a wreck on I-9 coming out of Houston, so we're running behind."

"Okay," he said with a long sigh. He glanced around the cab of the truck. "Do you have anything to drink? My mouth is dry as a Texas mudhole."

There was half a bottle of water in the cup holder. I took it out and handed it to him. "It's probably not cold," I said. I narrowed my eyes at the road ahead. Other than occasional car lights coming from the other direction, the road was dark as pitch as it wound through the Texas countryside.

"I think there's a little truck stop a couple of miles down," he said.

"How do you know that?" I asked.

He sighed and rubbed the sleep from his eyes. "Darlin', I've traveled this old road so many times I can tell you how many mailboxes there are between here and Calloway County."

"How many?" I asked, grinning without looking at him.

"Three hundred and twenty-two," he said. "Not counting the trailer park in Lynnville, which changes every time a twister comes through."

"You're so full of shit."

He chuckled and put a hand to his side.

"Does it hurt?" I asked.

"Only when I laugh," he said. He twisted the cap off the water bottle and chugged it down. Wiping his lips on the back of his hand, he nodded at the neon truck stop sign that appeared ahead.

"There it is," he said. "How about you buy me a burger for old time's sake."

I started to tell him to buy his own damn burger, but I made the mistake of glancing over while he was looking my way. Our eyes locked for a moment and it was almost like we were back at the lake in the cab of his old truck.

I felt an old familiar twitch between my legs.

My nipples plumped inside my bra.

I had to resist the urge to pull off on the side of the road and attack him.

I cleared my throat and turned on the blinker.

"All right," I said. "One burger for old time's sake."

Luke

I'd traveled this stretch of I-9 so many times I could do it with my eyes closed.

When you ride the rodeo circuit, you spend about eight seconds a week on the back of a bull if you're lucky, and the rest of the time getting to the next ride.

I usually came out in the top two or three at most events, which meant a trophy I didn't give a shit about and a few hundred dollars in prize money.

Take the top spot and they tossed in a silver belt buckle with a cowboy riding a bull or a bronco on it. I had a fucking glove box full of the damn things. Try paying your rent with a silver belt buckle.

The only one I gave two shits about was the one I was wearing when I was gored. I had earned it two years ago from the National Rodeo Association for being the top bull rider on the Texas circuit.

It wasn't worth much monetarily, but it had sentimental value to me. I took great pride in being the top bull rider that year; and not because it got me laid a lot by the cowgirls who kept up with such things.

It was proof that I hadn't wasted my time. And even though I barely earned enough to keep gas in the tank and food in my belly, I wouldn't trade my time on the circuit for anything.

When I started riding professionally six years ago, I had dreams of becoming the next Ty Murray, really the only guy ever to make a decent living as a rodeo rider. I quickly learned that I was no Ty Murray, but it was too late to turn back by then. I was addicted. I had bull riding shooting through my veins like a drug addict had heroin. I lived for those eight seconds of hanging on for dear life.

Now, with this gash in my side, I wondered if I'd ever climb back on a bull again. Over the years, I had suffered more concussions that most NFL players and had broken more bones than Evel Knievel. But

I'd never given a moment's thought to quitting. At least not before now. My brain was telling me it was time to hang up my spurs, but my heart was screaming bullshit. I reckoned all I could do was just wait and see which part of me won out.

"This looks like a great place to get food poisoning," Shelby said as she pulled into the lot, gravel crunching under the big tires. Mel's One Stop was a combination convenience store, greasy spoon diner, and ten-room motel.

The place looked like it had been there since Davy Crockett's time, but I knew from experience that Mel's had the best greasy hamburger in this part of Texas. I used to bang a waitress who worked there, a skinny gal with little tits and a tight box named Janine something or other. She'd give me free food and I'd give it to her hard and fast in the men's room. We both considered it a fair trade.

"It's a great place to get lots of things," I said as she parked us among the few pickups already in the gravel lot. I unbuckled the seat belt and held onto the door to slide out of the truck. I held on to the door for a moment till I got my sea legs.

I was a little wobbly at first, but I felt better than I had felt in a long time. Just getting out of that hospital seemed to do me a world of good. By the time Shelby came around the truck to see if I needed help, I had slammed the door and was managing to walk pretty well on my own.

"Hang on and let me help you," she said, clutching my arm. The moment her fingers touched my skin I felt little sparks shoot through my body like I'd stuck my finger in a light socket. I started to pull away and tell her I could do it myself, but I liked the way her hands felt on my arm.

"I'm just a little wobbly," I said, lying now so she wouldn't let go of me. I sniffed the air between us. She smelled of shampoo and soap, with just a hint of sweat. I used to spend hours licking the sweat off her naked body, like a kid licking an ice cream cone. The thought made my cock twitch a little. I quickly pushed the thought out of my mind. I wasn't wearing underwear and the last thing I needed was to walk into a truck stop with my big old pecker sticking out.

She opened the door and led me inside. We were greeted by stale air and the smell of grease. There were three cowboys at the counter, being served by an older waitress who told us to sit anywhere. Shelby led me to the farthest booth from the door and helped me get situated. She slid into the booth across from me and picked up the menu, which was just a half sheet of laminated paper with the choices written out in red magic marker.

"Well, apparently, they only serve burgers and fries," she said, a little condescendingly, like she expected the place to have fucking lobster and caviar on the menu. She held out the menu so I could see it. "What'll it be? A single, double, or a Mel's Special?"

"What's a Mel's Special?" I asked.

She read from the menu. "Three hamburger patties, three slices of American cheese, one fried egg, three strips of bacon, jalapeno peppers, lettuce, tomato, pickle... and a complimentary call to 911 after your heart seizes up."

The goofy look on her pretty face made me smile. I said, "I'll just have a single with fries and a Coke."

The waitress came over to take our order, then returned a minute later with two Cokes. She gave me a funny look, probably wondering where I had stolen the hospital scrubs from. Clearly, I was not a medical professional.

"So, how have you been?" I asked after taking a long sip of the Coke. It felt good going down my throat, which was still scratchy and sore from the breathing tube they'd shoved down it a week before. I let my eyes drift around her face. She was even prettier now than she was the last time I'd seen her.

"Better than you," she said, giving me the look. You know, *the look*: the look a woman gives a man when she's pissed about something, and then gets even more pissed that the man has no idea what she was pissed about in the first place.

She said, "You look like shit."

"Well, darlin', I happen to feel a little like shit at the moment," I said. I held my side and leaned over the table. "You wanna tell me what you're so mad about? I mean, Jesus, I haven't seen you in six years and rather than being glad to see me, you're acting like you're ready to bite my head off."

She folded her arms over her big boobs and glared at me. "You know very well why I'm mad at you."

I shook my head. "No, ma'am, I very well do not. Last time I saw you, things were fine between us. I haven't talked to you in six years. What the hell did I do to piss you off?"

She narrowed her eyes at me. "Maybe that's why I'm pissed."

I fell back in the seat and blew out a long sigh. Goddammit, trying to understand a woman was like trying to play piano with your toes: it was possible, but only a few people could do it and I wasn't one of them.

"Shelby, please, before I die, tell me what that means."

She huffed at me. She looked like she was ready to jerk me across the table and mop up the floor with me. In my weakened condition, there would not have been much I could have done to stop her.

The waitress brought our burgers over and set them in front of us. After a week of shitty hospital food, I thought the burgers smelled and looked delicious, but Shelby looked at hers like it was a trough of pig slop. I picked up the ketchup and squirted it all over my fries.

"When did you get so fuckin' snotty?" I asked, picking up three fries and swirling them through the ketchup before shoving them into my mouth.

"I'm not snotty," she said, picking up a limp fry and turning up her nose at it.

"You are, too, snotty," I said. "You act like you're too goddamn good to eat a greasy spoon hamburger."

"Maybe I am," she said with a shrug. She had removed the bun from her plate and set it aside. She had a knife and fork in her hands and was cutting up the hamburger patty and the slice of tomato in an equal number of bites. She stabbed a piece of tomato, then a piece of burger, and stuck them between her teeth. She didn't let her lips touch the fork, like she was afraid of catching anthrax or something. She chewed and stared at me.

I picked up the burger and took a huge bite. My guts were growling like a den of lions. It might have been my imagination, but as soon as the first bite slid down my gullet, the pain in my side started to ease. I sighed as I chewed, thinking I might just live after all.

"Why didn't you ever call me?" Shelby asked as she picked up her Coke and brought the straw to her lips. I watched her lips close around the straw, then her tongue slid slowly around her lips to clean them off. Goddamn if she still wasn't the sexiest little gal in the whole state of Texas. I felt my old pecker chubbing up a bit, just knowing she was sitting across the table from me.

"Why didn't I ever call you?" I asked. "Well, honestly, I figured you were too busy with school and I didn't want to bother you."

"Oh bullshit," she said, rolling her eyes.

"Why didn't you ever call me?" I asked, knocking that ball back into her court. "I mean, they must have had phones at that fancy cow college you went to. If you wanted to talk so goddamn bad you should have picked up the phone."

Her cheeks flushed and I knew I'd crossed a line. She still had the knife and fork in her hands. She aimed the knife at me like she was gearing up to throw it.

"I would have called you if I'd known how," she said. "You were always on the road. Nobody knew how to get hold of you, not even Cody. He said you didn't even had a cell phone."

"Cellphones cost money," I said, chomping off another big bite of the burger and chewing through the words. "I did good most weeks to have money for gas and food. I couldn't pay for a goddamn cellphone."

"You could have borrowed someone's phone," she said, shaking her head. She stabbed another bite of tomato and hamburger and waved them at me. "You should have called me."

"Okay, Shelby, I should have called you," I said with a defeated sigh. "I was just always on the road, traveling from one town to the next, trying to make a name for myself. I mean, I asked Cody for your number and he said he'd get it for me, but he never did."

"Oh, so it's Cody's fault that you're a selfish asshole," she said, rolling her eyes again. I swear, she was making me dizzy with all that eye rolling.

"No, goddammit, it's not Cody's fault," I said. "And who says I'm a selfish asshole?"

"Just everybody who's ever known you," she said, hands in the air, knife and fork waving like she was conducting some kind of greasy spoon orchestra. "You've always been a selfish asshole, Luke, ever since we were kids. And the sad thing was, me and Cody let you get by with it because we both loved you like a brother."

I blinked at her for a moment. I had never thought of myself as selfish. Truth was, I'd never thought about myself as anything other than a good old boy from Texas who appreciated a good cold beer, a good hard ride, and a nice tight piece of pussy. What was selfish about that?

"So, you're pissed at me because I haven't called you since we both left home," I said, nodding in slow comprehension. "Let me ask you something. Let's say I had called you. Exactly what would you have expected me to say?"

It was her turn to look at me like a dog watching a ceiling fan. "What you do mean?"

"I mean, did you expect me to say that everything was good and I was just checking in? Or that I missed you so much that it hurt? Or that I lay in the back of my truck many nights staring up at the stars and wishing you was lying next to me?" I huffed and spread out my hands. "I mean, seriously, Shelby, what did you want me to say?"

"Well, all of that, I guess," she said. All the air seemed to go out of her as she set back and put the knife and fork on the table. She had tears in her eyes. Goddammit, I hated it when a woman cried. She gazed into my eyes. "I reckon I wanted to just hear your voice."

I felt like a shit heel. I reached across the table and held out my hand. She put her hand in mine and my fingers closed around hers. "I never stopped thinking about you, Shelby," I said. "Not for one second. But the God's honest truth is, you and me, as much fun as we had, we had different takes on life. You wanted to get an education and build yourself a career that didn't include ranching and riding and shoveling shit. And I just wanted to ride bulls. I didn't want to force my dreams on you and I knew you well enough to know that you'd never force your dreams on me. So... well, I just figured if it was meant to be we'd come back around to each other one day."

She squeezed my hand. "And here we are."

"And here we are." I smiled and let my eyes go around her face. "And you ain't changed a bit."

"Oh bullshit," she said, tugging her hand away. She picked up her Coke and sucked on the straw. My eyes watched her lips purse, watched her suck on the straw. It was the first time in my life that I had been jealous of a damn straw.

"I mean it," I said, picking up my glass to toast her with it. "Shelby Cates is still the prettiest dang girl in the state of Texas. Period."

"Well, I think you might have sustained one too many concussions," she said. Her face went serious and she nodded at my side. "Seriously, how bad was it? And don't give me that 'I've had worse' bullshit."

"Well, I don't really remember getting gored." I leaned back and gently touched the bandage beneath the scrub shirt. "One minute I was on the back of the sumbitch and the next minute I was tossed in the air like a rag doll. Somebody said I came down on the bull's horn and he flung me around till he got tired and then tossed me aside. One of the cowboys that visited me in the hospital said there was a YouTube video of it, but I ain't seen it and have no desire to do so." I took a sip of Coke and set the glass on the table. "I mean, why would anyone wanna see themselves getting gored by a damned old bull? Not me."

"How bad was the damage?" she asked, a look of sadness in her pretty eyes.

"Well, it was considerable I guess," I said. "Punctured my stomach, ruptured my spleen, cracked a few ribs." I worked up a smile for her. "If you've never been gored, I do not recommend it. It can really fuck up your day."

"So how did you bust your stitches?" she asked, arching her eyebrows and giving me that look she always gave when we were kids and she caught me doing something I should have, like jacking off in the bathroom to her *Cosmo* magazine when I was fourteen.

"Like the nurse said, I got up by myself to take a leak and passed out on the floor."

"Why don't I believe you?" she asked, eyes rolling yet again.

"I do not know," I said, picking up the last chunk of my burger and stuffing it in my mouth. I smiled and chewed and smacked my lips. "You need to get your eyes checked. They seem to roll around an awful lot."

"Only when I'm around you," she said.

She picked up her fork and went back to work on her plate. I couldn't help but stare and wonder where we would be today if I hadn't gone off the ride the circuit and she hadn't gone off to college.

Would we have had a future together?

If so, would we still be together today?

Shelby wasn't the type to live on a ranch and pop out babies. And I wasn't the type to stay in one place for too long. No sir, whatever water had gone under the bridge between us was probably water well served. I seriously doubted even Shelby would have put up with my shit for this long.

Shelby

We sat and talked for what seemed like hours. I heard all about Luke's adventures on the rodeo circuit and bored him to death with highlights of my six years at A&M getting my Masters in agriculture. I want to work with seeds, I told him, developing wheat and rice seeds that would grow anywhere in the world, in any climate. It was a big goal, which flew right over his head.

"I'm not sure there's much call for that sort of thing, Shelby," he said, scratching at the stubble that covered his chin.

I frowned at him. "What do you mean?"

"Can't you just buy little packets of seeds at the Home Depot?" he asked with a shrug. "Or buy rice in a bag at the food mart?"

I couldn't tell if he was serious or not, but I was pretty sure he was. Lordy, how many times had this boy been dumped on his head?

We talked about home and horses and cattle and trucks and Cody and Daddy and Texas football. He asked if I was seeing anybody special and I just chuckled to avoid telling him he had more luck riding bulls than I had riding men.

I knew better than to ask if he was seeing anybody. The more accurate question would have been how many women was he seeing?

We did not talk about the number of women he'd been with or the number of men I'd had, although I was certain his count would far outnumber mine.

As I watched Luke shove the last of his fries into his mouth, I felt the anger that had festered inside me for so long slowly fading away. I had been pissed at him because he had never called me after he left home. I painted myself as the poor girl whom the hero left behind. But as he said, the truth was, I'd never ever tried to call him either. I said it was because I never knew where he was, but that wasn't entirely true.

Cody kept a pretty good track on Luke and told me several times that Luke was riding in rodeos near College Station where I was in school and around Houston just a short drive away.

I could have easily gone to see him if I'd wanted to, but I never did. Maybe Luke was right.

He didn't want to force his dreams on me and maybe I didn't want to force mine on him.

Or maybe I didn't know if I could resist just chucking my dreams to follow him around the rodeo circuit if he ever asked me to. I'd never had much willpower when it came to Luke Daniels.

Not as the little girl who followed him around like a lovesick pup.

Not as the teenager who spent many nights lying in his arms.

And not as the woman sitting across from him now, gazing into his eyes as little jolts of electricity arced across my nipples and little drops of joy-juice soaked into the crotch of my Victoria's Secret panties.

I glanced at the clock above the counter. "Holy crap, it's almost nine-thirty," I said. I glanced out the window. Yep, still dark. Duh. "We'd better get back on the road. We won't get home till after midnight at this rate."

Luke's lips curled into a smile. He nodded out the window. My eyes followed his gaze. He was looking at the motel office that sat cattycornered to the diner. The neon sign in the window read: VACANCIES.

He gave me a shrug and said, "We could just stay here tonight and head home in the morning. I mean, if you wanted to."

I slowly brought my eyes around to his. The air between us seemed to grow warm and moist, filled with electricity, like the air before a Texas thunderstorm.

I gave him a sympathetic look and said, "You do look tired."

His head slowly bobbed. "Yes, ma'am, it has been a long day."

"And your doctor would probably recommend that you get lots of bed rest."

"Yes, ma'am, I'm sure he would."

I glanced at his side as the warm juices started to flow freely between my legs. "Did the doctor say that you should avoid strenuous activity? I mean, I don't want you busting your stitches."

"The doc said I could do whatever I wanted to, so long as I was careful," he said seriously. "Physical activity in moderation is good, I think he said. And you know me. I'm all about the physical activity."

"Well then, doctor knows best," I said, reaching for my purse. I took out a twenty-dollar bill and set it on the table. "You pay our check. I'll get us a room."

Shelby

I led Luke to room 10 and opened the door. A wave of musty air rushed past us, as if it had been locked inside the room for years and couldn't wait for me to open the door so it could get free. I coughed and waved at the dust I'd kicked up just by opening the door, then reached inside the door and flicked on the light. A bedside lamp flickered to life.

"Well, it ain't much," I said, stepping aside to let Luke pass. "But we've both probably slept in worse."

"Who said anything about sleeping?" Luke asked with a grin. He held his side as he walked over to sit on the edge of the bed. He glanced around the room. "It's a shithole, but it's better than sleeping in the bed of a truck, which is where I spend most nights."

The room was standard issue roadside motel straight out of the 1970's. There was a double bed covered by a spread with a scenic cowboy riding a horse while roping a calf print. On the wall above the bed was a painting of a similar cowboy on a similar horse roping a similar calf. The spread and the painting had probably been in this room for decades.

There was a nightstand on one side of the bed with the lamp and an alarm clock that was off by several hours. A little round table and two chairs sat in front of the window, which was covered by heavy drapes the color of red wine. The air conditioner was beneath the window. I fiddled with the controls for a moment. It spat and sputtered, and finally made a noise like a diesel engine cranking to life and blew out air that was just slightly cooler than the thick air already in the room.

There was a rickety-looking dresser with an old, old, old television set sitting on top of a yellow doily that had probably once been white. The TV was so old it didn't even have a remote control or a cable running into the back of it. I could only assume that most people checking into Mel's Diner, Convenience Store, and Roadside Motel did not do so to watch TV.

I had bought a six-pack of Coors in the little store scotched between the motel office and diner. I set the cold beers on the dresser, then popped the top on two of them. I handed one to Luke and kept one for myself. I put the cold bottle to my lips as I walked over to the door leading into the bathroom and pushed it open with the toe of my boot.

Again, standard stuff; toilet, tub, shower; all relatively clean and free of traces from past visitors.

"You feel like a shower or a hot bath?" I asked. "No offense, but your hair looks like somebody plastered it to your head with a trowel." I noticed he was holding his side again. "Is it okay to get that wet?"

He tried to smile. I could tell it hurt. "The doc said I probably shouldn't get this wet for a few more days. I can shower, but I need to cover it with plastic somehow."

"Then we won't worry about a shower until we get you home and I can figure out how to wrap plastic around you or something."

"If you can get past the smell for tonight, that sounds like the best plan."

"I think I can manage." I took a long pull at the bottle and stared at him for a moment. I could barely believe I was in a shitty motel room with Luke Daniels, after all these years.

He was sitting on the edge of the bed with his feet on the floor and his hands on his knees. I had to smile because he looked so ridiculous in the hospital scrubs and cowboy boots.

He held out his arms and wiggled his fingers at me. "Come here."

I set the beer on the nightstand and moved to stand between his knees. He put his arms around my waist and pulled me toward him, resting his forehead between my breasts. He sighed as I wrapped my arms around his head and pulled him close. I rested my cheek on the top of his head.

"I've missed you, Shelby," he said quietly.

"I've missed you, too, Luke."

"I want to make love you," he said, looking up at me with dreamy eyes. "But I'm afraid I can't do much more than lie here."

"I think we can make that work," I said, putting my hands on his cheeks and lowering my lips to his. His lips were rough, but they were warm and his tongue was moist and when I stuck my tongue into her mouth so he could suck on it, the past came rushing back and I nearly came in my jeans.

God, how I'd missed the taste of this man.

I kissed him long and hard as his hands came around to undo my jeans. He hooked his thumbs into the waistbands of my jeans and panties and forced them down over my round ass and legs. I was still wearing my boots, so the jeans and panties gathered just below my knees.

I broke the kiss long enough to pull off my t-shirt and unhook my bra. When the bra slid down my arms, freeing my aching tits, Luke sighed his approval and cupped my tits in his hands. He kneaded my milky globes as his tongue said hi to my nipples, drawing circles around them, nipping with his teeth, sucking them between his lips.

"Get this off," I said, breathless already, tugging at his shirt. "Just raise your arms and I'll help you."

"Son of a bitch," he said, wincing as I pulled the shirt over his head and tossed it aside. I put my hands on his muscular shoulders and glanced down at this bandage. It was still clean, no sign of blood. I put my finger under his chin to lift it up so I could see his face. He was sweating a little, but his eyes were bright and he managed to give me a smile.

"We're gonna have to be careful," I said. "I don't want you to do anything to pop those stitches. I'd hate to have to call the cook to sew you up."

"I'll be fine," he said as his hands slid from my breasts to my ass. He flexed his fingers into the soft flesh of my ass and let his little fingers slide down to tease my asshole. He glanced down at the neat patch of curls pointing toward my clit. "Maybe I can just lay back and you can just do a slow ride, like in the good old days."

"Hmm, I can do that," I said, kissing him again.

He kept squeezing my ass with his left hand, then brought his right hand around to slide between my legs. I spread my thighs so he could slide his fingers across my sopping pussy, lubing them up so they would slide easily inside me.

He began fucking me with one finger while his thumb rolled my clit from side to side. I was two seconds away from cumming all over his hand. It had been awhile since I'd been touched by a man down there. Especially a man I cared about. Luke's fingers were hitting all the switches, turning on my water works, sending shudders of orgasm throughout my body.

"Fuck... I'm gonna... cum... already..."

Luke started thrusting his fingers in and out of my pussy at a faster pace. He put his lips to my nipple and sucked hard as his other hand dug into my ass cheeks. I got on my tiptoes and pulled his head into my chest and came in a downpour, washing over his hand like a torrential Texas thunderstorm.

I'd always been a gusher. When I cum I shoot juice out of my pussy like water through a firehose. As Luke rammed his fingers as deep inside of me as they'd go, I came in great bursts, showering his hand with a flow of hot juices that splashed all over the insides of my thighs and dripped to the floor.

My sudden release of juices and the smell that filled the air made Luke moan in delight. He looked up at me and smiled. "I'd forgotten what a mess you always made," he said, planting kisses across my breasts. "Remember how we used to sleep on towels because you'd get the bed so wet?"

"I remember," I moaned, still trying to catch my breath. His fingers were still inside me. I wiggled my pussy against his hand and flicked my tongue across his lips. "I remember how you used to shoot a load in the air like a water fountain when I pumped you hard with my hand. Do you still do that?"

He grinned at me. "Why don't we find out?"

As I went to the bathroom to get a warm washcloth, Luke shimmied out of his boots and scrub pants and lay back on the bed with his head on the pillows and his legs spread wide. I gasped a little when I saw his monster cock for the first time in years. I had forgotten how long and thick it was, almost like one of those big foot-long silicon dildos you can order off the internet (or so I hear).

His cock stuck straight up from his curly pubes like a flag pole ready for a salute. I felt juices flowing again in anticipation of having his cock in my hands, in my mouth, and especially, in my pussy.

Luke

Just feeling Shelby's hot juices gushing over my hand was enough to make me nearly blow a load myself. I had somehow forgotten that she was a gusher.

In the old days, I'd lie on my back and she'd straddle that sweet pussy over my mouth and I would suck and probe and lick until she came like a roaring hurricane, gushing hot juice all into my mouth and all over my face.

It tasted like hot sweet tea.

I would swallow and lick and swallow and suck and swallow some more until I got every last drop of it out of her. Then I'd lay her down and fuck her like there was no tomorrow.

Shelby went to wash herself off while I got naked on the bed. I pulled myself back onto the pillows with my elbows. My fucking side was burning like a thousand bee stings, but I did not care. I was with Shelby. I was about to feel her hands and mouth and pussy on my big old cock. That was all I cared about at that moment. You could have chopped off my arm with a dull hatchet and my cock would not have gone down. There was only one way to release the blood pumping in that monster and that was with Shelby's help.

"Holy shit, that damn thing's just gotten bigger," Shelby said, coming out of the bathroom with a washcloth between her hands. She spread her legs and gave her cooch a good wipe down, then tossed the rag on the bed and slid in beside me.

"He's missed you, too," I said, forcing a smile. I put my hands behind my head and ignored the pain in my side. "Why don't you say hello?"

Shelby lay on the bed next to me in the opposite direction, with her knees bent and thighs spread so I could work my fingers back into her pussy while she worked her magic on my cock. She braced on her right elbow so her right hand could play with my balls, then took my cock in her left hand and hovered her mouth over it.

"Well, hello, big man," she cooed, blowing her hot breath on the head of my cock as her fingers closed around the lower half of the shaft. I tensed my groin muscles and the head blossomed for her. Little drops of juice appeared at the slit. Shelby eagerly licked them off with the tip of her tongue.

My fingers slid into Shelby's pussy, still hot and bubbly and flowing like the Rio Grande. I had really long fingers. I bunched three of them together and slowly started fucking her with them while my thumb massaged her clit. Shelby took the head of my cock into her mouth and moaned.

"Damn... girl... you sure... know how to... say hello..." I sighed, closing my eyes, reveling in the feel of her lips and hand on my cock. She took the head into her mouth and sucked it like hard candy as her hand slid up and down the foot-long shaft. She leaned my cock back and pressed her lips and tongue to the underside and worked them up and down. Goddammit, I'd missed this girl. I'd had a lot of blowjobs in my day, but nobody could suck my dick like Shelby Cates. She was a goddamn grandmaster cocksucker if there ever was one. She deserved a silver championship buckle, if they gave away buckles for such things.

"Your cock... is so... fucking huge..." she hummed with the head between her lips.

"And your pussy is so fucking wet..." I said, driving my fingers knuckle deep inside her and wiggling them around. "I want to fuck you, Shelby. Get on top of me and fuck me slow like the old days."

"With pleasure," she said, wiggling herself free of my fingers and moving to straddle her hot pussy over my long cock. We gave each other a nostalgic grin. We'd done this position many times before, starting with the night Cody caught us fucking in the barn loft on Shelby's sixteenth birthday.

My cock was too big to fit inside her all the way, so she couldn't just climb on like a horse and ride the thing like a fuckin' buckin' bronco. She could only take part of it inside her, but it was enough to get both our nuts off and leave us more than satisfied.

I held my cock steady at the base as she lowered her pussy onto it. She paused for a moment with the head pushed against her hole. I swirled the head around to juice it up good, then took some juice on my free hand and lubed up the part of the shaft that would fit inside her.

She lowered herself onto me, just enough to let the head slide inside her. I could literally feel her tight pussy stretching to take me in. Holy fucking shit, I won't lie. I almost shot my load right then and there. I blew out a long breath and held it back.

"Fuck... you're huge..." she said, lowering herself onto the shaft by an inch, then another. I was probably five or six inches inside her when I felt the tip of my cock hit her back wall. I had plenty more to go, but that was all she could safely get inside her. I had yet to meet a woman who could take my entire cock inside her pussy, though there was this little gal in Abilene who could take it all down her throat and never gag. She was like a goddamn sword swallower at a freak show. Not much to look at, but holy cow...

I wrapped my fingers around the part of my cock not inside her and gave her a smile. "Now," I said. "Ride your pony."

Shelby clutched her hands to her tits and started rolling her hips back and forth, sliding her pussy over the six inches of cock inside her. I squeezed the base to keep the end she was fucking engorged and hard for her. Each time her pussy took me inside her, her clit would brush against my thumb and she'd jump like she was being shocked by an electric fence.

"Holy... fucking shit... that feels... amazing," she sighed, pinching her nipples so hard they turned purple between her fingers. I just watched her with a joy in my heart that I had not felt in a very long time.

She closed her eyes and darted her tongue across her lips. Her nostrils flared each time her pussy drove down the length of cock inside her. I could have cum right then myself, just from watching her, but I held off.

I knew how Shelby wanted the round to end.

I would not take that enjoyment away from her.

"Oh... fuck... I'm gonna... cum..." she said, her hips thrashing faster, impaling her sweet pussy hard on my cock and against my hand.

"Cum for me, baby," I said. "Cum hard for old Luke."

She screamed and jackhammered against my hand. I watched her face as she came. She squeezed her eyes shut and gritted her teeth. She thrashed her head from side to side, her long ponytail whipping like a mare's tail running across an open field.

"God... damn... fuck... me... Luke... fuck... your big cock..."

I smiled. I always said Shelby talked out of her head when she came. She never believed me. Maybe one day I'd record it to prove it to her. I mean, if I ever got the chance again.

She gushed her hot juices all down my cock and over my hand and balls. I loved it and used her lube to pump my cock, keeping it hard for her until she finished cumming. After a moment, she caught her breath and smiled down at me.

"Can I milk you?" she asked.

"He's all ready for you," I said. "Lubed up with your juices."

Shelby lifted herself off my cock and sat between my legs Indian-style. My cock was still rock hard, covered in her glistening goo. The head was the size of a lemon and the color of a plum. Veins the size of red wigglers ran the length of the shaft. The damn thing looked like it was about to blow.

"I saved it for you," I said, putting my hands behind my head. I know what you want to do."

"Yes," she hissed, wrapping the fingers of both hands around my shaft and pumping them slowly up and down, like she was churning butter. Shelby loved to make me cum with her hands and mouth. She loved seeing me shoot my hot seed in the air like lava erupting out of the top of a volcano. I liked to cum inside her, but this was her favorite thing to do.

"That's it," she said, her hands sliding up and down. "Get really hard for me." She pressed her lips to the tip and swirled her tongue around the slit. "Cum for Shelby, baby. Cum for me."

She was panting as heavily as I was. She was playing with my balls with one hand, pumping the entire length of my shaft with the other, and sucking on the head with her luscious lips. Fuck, I couldn't hold it any longer. I curled my toes and flexed the muscles in my legs and moaned.

"I'm cummin'... fuck... Shelby... I'm cummin' hard..."

Shelby's eyes grew wide and her hand on my cock quickened its pace. She hovered her mouth a few inches over the tip of my cock and pumped that monster for all it was worth.

"Fuck... I'm gonna blow..."

I came like Old Faithful, shooting the first wave of my hot seed across her lips and into her eager mouth. She leaned back licking her lips and pumped her hand faster, knowing there was more to come. A long rope of milky jizz shot six inches into the air and fell on her hands just as another gush followed behind it.

"Oh... fuck... I'm cumming again..." Shelby said. She had started rubbing her clit when I told her I was cumming. She closed her eyes and moaned. She had my cum on her lips and her cum on her hand. She was in fucking heaven and so was I.

She pumped and sucked my cock until there was nothing more to give. We ended up a sticky mess. I had my milky goo all over my cock and balls and stomach. She had it on her face and her hands and the bed beneath her ass was drenched with her warm juices.

Just like old times.

We just looked at each other and grinned.

Shelby handed me the wet rag she'd left lying on the bed, then padded off to the bathroom to take a shower.

I cleaned myself off as best I could and fell back on the pillows, completely exhausted. I had momentarily forgotten about the pain in my side because all the blood was busy in my groin. But as my body slowly came back to earth, the pain returned.

I closed my eyes and took a few deep breaths, hoping to push the pain away in case Shelby wanted to go for round two when she got out of the shower.

I was fighting a losing battle.

My body was spent.

The pain was my brain's way of telling me to behave myself and go to fucking sleep.

The rest of me was too tired to argue, so reluctantly, that's what I did.

Shelby

I woke up to find Luke sitting in the chair at the little round table in front of the window. He was already dressed in his blue scrubs and cowboy boots, drinking coffee from a tall Styrofoam cup.

There was a second cup there, also his because I don't drink coffee, along with what looked like a wrapped biscuit of some kind and a can of Mountain Dew.

Aw, how sweet.

Luke remembered that I was a Mountain Dew fanatic.

If I didn't have a can of Mountain Dew first thing in the morning I was like an angry bear coming out of hibernation.

I stretched out my arms and yawned at him. "Morning," I said, giving him a sleepy smile. "Whatcha got there?"

"Morning, sleepy head," he said. He popped the top on the Mountain Dew and set it on the nightstand, then sat on the bed and unwrapped what turned out to be a convenience store biscuit and sausage.

"As I recall, you're as mean as a bobcat if you don't have your Mountain Dew first thing in the morning. And I got you this to make sure you started your day off with the government recommended allowance of breakfast grease."

"You're so sweet," I said, sitting up in the bed with the covers up to my belly button and my titties hanging out. My nipples were plump and red, and a little sore from the previous night's fun. But they were glad to see Luke again. He made them very happy.

I took a good long drink of the Mountain Dew, but told him to eat the nasty biscuit and sausage. I wasn't a big breakfast person, but obviously he was. He made short work of the biscuit and fetched the second cup of coffee from the table to wash it down.

"Cody called," he said, blowing into the steaming cup.

"He did? When?"

"About half an hour ago." He nodded at my cellphone, which was lying on the nightstand. "I didn't want to wake you up, so I just answered it."

I licked Mountain Dew from my lips and arched my eyebrows at him. "What did you tell him?"

"The truth," he said with a shrug. "That we were late getting out of the hospital and there was a wreck on I-9. By the time we stopped for dinner my side was hurting something fierce and you were horny as a three-peckered billy goat, so you insisted that we get a room in a shithole motel so you could give me a little physical therapy."

My mouth dropped open. "You did not."

"I did," he said, trying to keep from smiling. "I told him you were especially good at oral therapy and that as long as I had a face, you had a place to sit."

"You're awful," I said, swatting at him. He slid his hand under the sheet and let his fingers slide up my thigh. I spread my legs for him and sighed when the tips of his fingers reached their destination. "What... did you... really tell him?"

"I just told him we were running late and we'd be on our way soon as I had a bite to eat."

His fingers slid inside my wet pussy. He rolled my clit under his thumb, making me moan. I threw back the sheet and spread my legs for him.

"Well then," I said, panting. "I reckon you better eat so we can get on the road."

Luke

We rolled into Calloway County around noon and turned onto the mile-long gravel drive that led to Shelby's Daddy's house fifteen minutes later. I leaned in to look through the windshield at the big iron gates as we drove through. The letters CCR for Cate's Cattle Ranch were displayed in a decorative circle of metallic rope in the arch that loomed over the drive.

Shelby wasn't in a hurry. She had her left wrist draped over the steering wheel and right arm resting on the console, driving casually, like she had no particular place she had to be at no particular time. We'd a had a great time just chatting away like old friends—old lovers—happy to have rekindled our acquaintance and romance.

Neither one of us talked about what would happen when I was well enough to go back to riding the circuit and she found a job doing whatever it was her degree qualified her to do.

I just knew whatever she did, it would not include following me around or living on a dirt farm somewhere raising a bunch of rug rat kids.

Shelby wasn't meant for that kind of life.

She was destined for greater things, like doing something with seeds to feed the world (I guess?), and there was no way in hell that I was gonna stand in her way.

Cody and Alvin Lee, Shelby's Daddy, were sitting on the front porch waiting for us when we pulled up the drive. I hadn't seen either of them in years. Cody looked pretty much the same as the last time I saw him. Big, handsome, broad-shouldered, with skin the color of saddle leather and eyes the color of a crow's wings.

Alvin Lee, on the other hand, who had always been a great bear of a man, had put on a little weight around the middle and his bushy mustache and hair had gone to salt and pepper. He still had a twinkle in his eye and a smile on his lips. And I knew he could probably still out-ride, out-rope, and out-fuck me and Cody even on our best days.

Shelby shoved the gear into Park and yelled out the window at them. "Be careful with him. He's got stitches that might bust."

"You didn't seem so concerned last night," I said quietly, so only she could hear. She grinned and told me to shut up.

My door opened and Alvin Lee was standing there with his arms out. He waited until I slid out of the truck, then gave me a careful hug.

"I'll be damned, it's good to have you home," he said, giving me a careful hug. He took a step back and huffed at my outfit. "Holy hell, boy, they couldn't send you home in big boy clothes?"

"Hell, I had to pretend to be a doctor just to get out of the place," I said, slapping him on the shoulder.

Cody brushed past his Daddy and stuck out his hand. "Just shake my hand, you old sumbitch. I don't wanna pop your stitches."

"How you been, brother?" I asked, giving his hand a slowly shake.

"I been better than you," Cody said. "Pull up your shirt and let me see your battle scars."

I winced as I tugged up my shirt to show him the bandage. I saw him frown and looked down to see a spot of red the size of a baseball on the center of the gauze.

"Shit," I said, suddenly a little swimmy-headed. "They said it might bleed. I just need to change the bandage."

"I'll do that," Shelby said, coming around the truck and sliding under my left arm. She put her arm around my back and barked orders at Cody. "Get the door. Help me get him to his old room. I'll get some fresh bandages."

"Yes, ma'am," Cody said, giving me a wink. "Some things never change."

"That's good to know," I said, giving Shelby a little squeeze. I put my lips to her ear as she helped me up the stairs. "Can I sleep in your room."

"Uh, not unless you want to add a shotgun wound to your list of ailments," she said, cutting me a sideways glance. "Daddy still thinks we're little kids. If he knew what you'd been doing to his little girl..."

"Cody is right," I said, glancing over my shoulder at Cody and Alvin Lee, who were just a couple of steps behind us. "Some things never change."

Shelby

Cody got Luke settled into his old bed in his old room on the second floor while I found clean gauze and bandages in the pantry in the kitchen. This was a working cattle ranch.

There was always somebody getting scraped, cut, burned, stomped, or worse. Most of the men working the ranch were tough as nails cowboys who could cut off a finger and not even skip a beat.

The bandages were left over from when I was a kid. If I so much as scraped a knee or got a bee sting Daddy acted like it was the end of the world. He was always protective of his little girl. And watching him give me and Luke the eye told me that he had not lightened up one bit. He was glad to have Luke home, but he'd run him off in a heartbeat if he knew what we did behind his back.

I took the bandages, tape, scissors, and a bottle of Peroxide that had expired a year before into Luke's bedroom. Luke was lying back on the pillows with the sheet up to his waist and his eyes closed. The scrub shirt was off already, lying on the floor. His muscular chest rose and fell gently as I quietly entered the room. For a moment, I thought he was asleep.

Luckily, the bloody spot on the bandage had not gotten bigger.

I sat down on the side of the bed and tugged at the corners of the tape holding the bandage to Luke's skin.

"Your hands are cold," he said, opening one eye to smile at me.

"I'm sorry," I said, cupping my hands and blowing into them.

He chuckled, winced. "I'm just messing with you." He set his hand on my thigh and scratched his dirty nails to my jeans. "Thank you for taking care of me."

"Don't thank me until you see what kind of nurse I am," I said. I sucked in a breath and held it as I slowly stripped the tape from his skin. Luke closed his eyes and breathed deeply in and out.

I peeled the damp bandage from the wound. I swallowed hard when I saw the gash in his side. I'd never been good at this sort of thing. The sight of blood usually made me sick. True to form, I felt nauseous and sweaty, like I was gonna throw up all over his beautiful chest.

"You okay?" he asked.

I took a deep breath and gave him a little nod, and swallowed back the taste of vomit that was burning at my throat. "Yep, I'm fine. Just hold still."

He had a line of stitches holding together an incision six inches long that ran down his left side and across the left side of his stomach. The stitches were caked with dried blood and the incision was fiery red. The blood had seeped through the gash at the center.

"Does it hurt?" I asked, knowing it was a stupid question.

"Only when I breathe," he said, forcing a smile for my benefit. He closed his eyes and blew out a long breath. "Just do what you gotta do and get it over with."

I opened the bottle of Peroxide and soaked a cotton ball, then dabbed the cotton ball to the stitches and gash to wash away the blood. I tried to be careful because each time Luke winced or sucked in a quick breath it made me jerk my hand back.

"Don't be such a baby," I said as I doused a clean cotton ball with Peroxide and finished cleaning off the blood. I leaned in and squinted at the stitches. "The bleeding's stopped, but you still need to take it easy."

"Does that mean no more hanky-panky for a while?" he asked, his fingers scratching their way toward my crotch, which was so warm I thought my panties had caught fire. I slapped his hand away.

"That's exactly what it means," I said. I playfully put my hand on the sheet covering his cock, which was draped lazily across his thigh like a snake sleeping on a rock. It jumped at my touch.

"You're going to have to keep the monster in his cage, at least for a few days."

He leaned back and sighed. "Shit. Okay. You're the boss."

"Yes, I am," I said, scraping a fingernail down his cheek. "After you rest for a while maybe you can take a shower and get a shave."

"You ever shave a man before?" he asked.

I glanced toward the door to make sure we were alone, then leaned in to give him a kiss. "No, but I've done a lot of firsts with you. I'm sure I can figure out how to shave you without cutting your throat."

I redressed the wound, gave him four Tylenol and a bottle of water, and told him to go to sleep.

By the time I had gathered up the old bandages, his eyes were closed and he was snoring like a baby.

Shelby

Cody was sitting at the kitchen table when I came back downstairs. He was finishing off one of his famous bologna, cheese, dill pickle, mustard, and potato chip sandwiches, and drinking a tall glass of iced tea.

"He okay?" he asked as I stuffed the bloody bandages into the trash can and went to the sink to wash my hands.

"I think he will be if we can keep him off the back of a damn bull," I said, shaking my head. "I swear, I will never see the attraction in bull riding. It's just insanely dangerous. I hope this convinces him to give it up for good."

"It's what he does, Shelby," Cody said, wiping his mouth on the back of his hand. "It's who he is. I guarantee you that soon as he's healed, he'll be out there in the corral looking for something to ride."

"Not if I have anything to say about it," I said. I opened the fridge and took down a glass from the cupboard. I dropped in a few ice cubes, then filled the glass with sweet tea and moved to sit down across the table from Cody.

"If you have anything to say about it?" Cody probed his back teeth with his tongue and gave me a hard look. "Since when do you have any say in what Luke does or does not do? You haven't seen him in six years."

I took a sip of tea and shrugged my eyebrows. "I don't have a say, necessarily. But he almost died and I intend to remind him of that until he gets it through his thick head that riding bulls is gonna be the death of him." I glanced out the open kitchen door. "Where's Daddy?"

"Daddy's already gone back to work," Cody said, leaning into the table and cocking his head at me. He stared at me for a moment, like he was trying to see through me.

"What?" I asked.

"What did you do, Shelby?" he asked.

"What do you mean?"

"I mean what did you do?"

"I didn't do anything."

He lifted his chin to look me in the eye. "What happened last night?"

I tried to feign ignorance, but it was no use. Cody had always been able to work the truth out of me.

I said, "We were in a motel, all right. Is that okay with you? We are consenting adults, you know. What we do is none of your business."

Cody spread out his big hands like he was releasing a pair of doves into the air. "I don't give a good goddamn that you two are fucking again, Shelby," he growled. "What I care about is the fact that Luke hasn't been home ten minutes and you're already back trying to control his life."

"That's bullshit," I snapped, giving him a hard frown. "I'm just trying to keep him safe."

"No, Shelby, you're not. You're doing exactly what you did six years ago, and if you're not careful, things are gonna end up the same way and you won't see him for another six years. Maybe more this time."

I blinked at him. "What the fuck are you talking about?"

"You wanted to go to A&M and Luke wanted to ride the rodeo circuit," Cody said, leaning back and folding his arms over his chest. "You pestered the living hell out of him. You wanted him to move to College Station and enroll in classes and play house with you."

"I did not." Yes, I did, but I didn't want to admit it to him.

"You harped on the boy until he was almost ready to do it, too," Cody said, head bobbing. "He came to me and said he was gonna give it a try just to make you happy. Fuck, Shelby, the boy barely graduated high school and you wanted him to apply to A&M? He wasn't gonna get into A&M. And if he had, he would have been miserable because he put his dreams on hold for you."

"He could have gone to the community college there," I said. "Or the tech school. He could have made something of himself and be earning a good living now."

"Doing what? Working as a mechanic at the Ford dealership? Or crawling under houses running fucking sewer pipes? Do you seriously think that would have made him happy?"

"I would have made him happy," I said, though it didn't come out as convincing as I'd hoped. "Besides, if he had come away with me he wouldn't be upstairs right now with a big gash in his side."

"No, he'd probably be somewhere working his ass off at some shit job he hated just to pay you child support."

"You're such an asshole," I said, gritting my teeth, trying not to cry.

"And you're such a selfish little girl."

"Fuck you, Cody."

"Fuck you, Shelby."

I clenched my jaws and looked away from him. I wiped my eyes with the tips of my fingers and shook my head. "I can't believe you're acting like this. Such an asshole."

Cody huffed a heavy sigh and flattened his palms on the table like he was bracing himself against a stiff wind. He said, "I'm gonna tell you something, Shelby, and I know you're gonna be pissed, but you need to know the truth."

"What truth?" I asked, dreading his answer, though I didn't know why.

"He was gonna go with you," Cody said quietly. "He came to me and said he was gonna forget about riding bulls so he could go to College Station with you."

I blinked at him through the tears. "He was?"

"Yes, he was."

I took a deep breath. I didn't know why, but my hands were starting to shake. I wrapped my fingers around the tea glass to keep them still. "What did you tell him?"

Cody looked me in the eye. "I told him he was a goddamn fool if he was gonna put his dreams on hold to help you chase yours."

My jaw fell open. "You what?"

"I told him that if he went with you to College Station, he would be miserable. And he would have made you miserable. I told him the best thing he could do was to pack up his shit and hit the circuit and let you go to college."

"What... how dare you..."

"I knew y'all loved each other, but your dreams were set too far apart. You were chasing different stars, Shelby, in different parts of the sky. And it wasn't fair for you to expect him to put his dreams on hold just because you didn't want to be alone."

"Oh my god..." I said, putting my hands to my cheeks. "What gave you the right? How dare you interfere in my life?"

"I told you that you were gonna be pissed," Cody said with a shrug. He popped the last bite of sandwich into his mouth and chewed for a moment, then drained the tea glass to wash it down. He got up from the table to set his dishes in the sink.

"Don't you leave," I said, seething at him. My face must have been red as a beet because I could feel the blood pumping through my brain. "I'm not done talking to you yet."

"Well, I'm done talking to you," Cody said. He dug two fingers into the pocket of his shirt and brought out a slip of paper and handed it to me.

"What is this?" I asked, opening the paper which had a name and phone number on it.

"That guy called yesterday," Cody said. "About a job you applied for before you came home."

"Oh my god," I muttered, recognizing the name as the corporate recruiter from Monsanto I'd met with a few months before. Monsanto was the largest producer of seeds in the country. Working in their research lab was my dream job. The job was in Houston, three hours away.

"Don't do it again, Shelby," Cody said as he plucked his dusty hat off the rack by the back door and set it on his head. "Don't try to make him choose your dream over his. This time, you might not get him back."

Shelby

I waited until Cody was out the door and headed toward the barn before getting up to find my cell phone. I was so mad at him I could have chewed nails, but I'd have to deal with him later. Right now, my attention was on the slip of paper in my hand.

I found my cell phone in my purse by the front door and took into Daddy's study, which was what he called the small room off the foyer that held a worn red leather chair older than me, a side table with his pipe, tobacco pouch, and silver lighter in the shape of a western pistol, and a big glass ashtray that always seemed to need emptying.

There was a brass floor lamp with a dusty shade and a wall of shelves that held a couple thousand western novels by Zane Grey, Louis L'Amour, Larry McMurtry, and other authors I'd never heard of.

I closed the door, sat on the edge of the chair, and punched in the number. I cleared my throat a dozen times as the phone rang. A receptionist answered and I asked for Ted Pruitt.

"Hi, Mr. Pruitt, this is Shelby Cates. I had a message that you had called yesterday." I listened for a moment, almost hoping that he was just calling to tell me that there was no place for me at Monsanto. I'd just gotten Luke back in my life. It was too soon to let life tear us apart again.

"Yes, sir, that's wonderful news, of course I accept. Yes, please email me the offer letter and I'll sign it and send it back immediately. Yes, sir, a week from Monday sounds fine. Thank you, sir. Thank you."

I hung up the phone and put a hand over my heart.

It felt like it was gonna beat right out of my chest.

Shit. I mean, yay!

My dream job had just become a reality.

Today was Friday.

A week from Monday I'd start my career as a research scientist at Monsanto's Houston labs, doing research and development on new seed hybrids.

I couldn't wait to tell Luke.

Surely, he'd want to come with me.

Luke

The day we got back to the ranch I slept almost fifteen hours straight. Cody said Shelby was so worried that she kept coming in to check on me to make sure I was still breathing.

When I finally managed to pry my eyes open and my ass out of bed, she wrapped plastic wrap around my waist and over my bandages so I could take a shower. I felt like a damned convenience store burrito. It was all I could do to resist pulling her into the shower with me. I would have loved to have soaped up her big titties and fucked her from behind as the hot water sprayed down on us. Sadly, that would be a fantasy we'd have to play out another day, when her Daddy and his shotgun weren't around.

It was kind of nice showering alone, though. Taking my time, letting the hot water jets beat against my sore shoulders and neck. Fuck, just getting a week's worth of hospital grime and sex goo off me made me feel a hundred times better.

I spent the next few days in bed most of the time, but slowly started moving around the house. Shelby refused to let me do much other than move from bed to kitchen chair to porch swing to bed. She fed me like a damn horse, insisting that I eat every bite of food she put in front of me.

Finally, I felt good enough to get out of bed for most of the day. I borrowed some of Cody's clothes and underwear and socks. I'd lost a considerable amount of weight, so Cody's clothes hung on me like a set of bad drapes. Shelby had to help me pull on my boots, but other than that I managed on my own.

The scar was healing well and the pain was subsiding, although I still had to be careful because sometimes the pain would hit out of nowhere and hitch me over double for a minute or two. I recalled the doc telling me that anytime they worked on your insides, it could take months, if not years, to completely heal. Screw that. I didn't have years to lay on my ass. I wasn't getting no younger.

I didn't mention it to Shelby, but I planned to be back on a bull soon as the rodeo season started again in a few months.

I didn't mention it because I knew she would go through the roof.

She kept making these little comments about how dangerous bull riding was, and how I wasn't getting no younger, and how I ought'a be thinking about my long-term future.

I let the comments go, partially because I didn't have the strength yet to argue with her and partially because I knew she was right.

Bull riding was dangerous and I wasn't getting no younger.

And I rarely thought past my next ride.

But goddammit, I wasn't ready to just roll over and die.

At least not yet.

* * *

I was sitting at the kitchen table nursing a cup of coffee when the screen door opened and Alvin Lee came in, wiping sweat off his face with the sleeve of his shirt. A cloud of dust followed him in. He hung his hat on the rack by the door and gave me the eye.

"How you feeling, boy?" he asked. He went to the sink and washed his hands, then opened the fridge and pulled out a bottle of water. He twisted off the cap and took the chair next to me.

"I'm better every day," I said with my hand on my side. "I'll be out there riding and roping with you and Cody before you know it."

"Don't rush it," he said, shaking his head with the bottle at his lips. He wiped his bushy mustache with his fingers. "Worse thing you can do is get back on a horse or a bull too soon and have your guts pop out in the middle of the arena."

"Yes, sir, that's the truth." I smiled and gave him little a nod. I held my coffee cup between my hands and stared into it. I didn't want to look him in the eye because I had the fear that he would see guilt all over my face. I had done nasty things to his little girl and I knew that he would see that in my eyes. I could tell he was watching me. I could feel his steel blue eyes burning into my face like a hot branding iron.

"So, Luke, what's you plan?" he asked, sitting back with the water resting on his chest.

I glanced up and shrugged. "Reckon I'll heal up and get back on the road."

"No, son, I mean what's your plan regarding Shelby?"

I glanced up again and my eyes locked on his. I tried not to blink. "Sir?

"I asked what's your plan regarding Shelby."

"Um, well, I'm not sure I understand the question."

He huffed and shook his head at me. "Son, do you think I'm stupid?"

"No, sir," I said quickly. "You're probably the smartest man I know."

He chucked and rubbed a knuckle under his nose. "Son, if that's the case you need to greatly widen your social circle." He grinned at me for a moment, then put his elbows on the table and leaned in over them. "I know about you and Shelby. I always have."

I blinked at him. "You have?"

"I have. I also know she's been head over heels for you since she was a teenager," he said, cutting his eyes at me. "And I expect you've always had feelings for her. At least I hope you have. I'd hate to think that you were just using her." He gave me a moment to respond. I didn't know what to say, so I just nodded and hoped it would suffice.

"I was young once, I know the things that teenagers do," he said with a heavy sigh. "And I also know the things that grownups do."

"I'm not sure I understand," I said. My eyes went around the room, looking for a shotgun that might be leaning in a corner.

"I mean y'all are not teenagers anymore," he said, the humor draining from his face to make room for a scowl that made me lean back in my chair. "Y'all can't just run off to the barn to fool around and then get back to business anymore. Teenagers have hormones. Adults have feelings." He narrowed his eyes at me again. "You get my meaning now?"

"Yes, sir," I said, swallowing hard. "I believe so."

"So, I'll ask you again. What's your plan regarding Shelby?"

I blew out a long sigh and spread my hands. "I'm not sure I have a plan." A sharp pain bit at my guts. I put a hand to my side and tried not to wince. "I mean, to be honest with you, I didn't expect to need a plan until I saw her walk into that hospital room a few days ago."

Alvin Lee's head bobbed, like he understood. He was an old cowboy. He'd ridden the circuit back in the day. He understood the lure of the road and the ride. But he also understood the love of a good woman, even though it was something he'd never really had.

He finished off the bottle of water and set it aside, then brushed the knuckle across his lips and gave me a firm look. "I'm just gonna say one thing on the subject and then I'll shut up," he said. "If you love her, hang on to her for dear life because there ain't too many women like Shelby. But if you're just messing with her to pass the time, well, son, it would be best if you heal up and move on quick as you can."

"Yes, sir, I understand."

He got up from the table, plucked his hat off the rack and worked it between his hands for a moment. He set his hand on the screen door, but paused before pushing it open.

"I reckon you know that if you break her heart you'll have to answer to me," he said without looking back at me.

"Yes, sir," I said. "I understand."

"All right then." He set the hat on his head, pushed open the screen, and went out the door.

I blew out a long breath and rubbed my eyes.

What was my plan regarding Shelby?

I had no fucking clue.

Shelby

It was Wednesday already and I hadn't mentioned the Monsanto job to Luke, even though I had to leave on Sunday. I had told Cody about the job and made him swear that he wouldn't say a word, not even to Daddy, who would want to make a big deal over it.

"You ain't told Luke yet?" Cody asked as we stood at the sink washing the dinner dishes. I glanced out the window over the sink. Luke was moving around pretty good now, getting out of bed and walking around the house, sitting on the porch. I could see him standing at the corral with Daddy, their long arms draped over the top rail, shoulder to shoulder, chatting like old pals. They were watching one of the cowboys trot a new pony around the corral.

"I'll tell him when the time is right," I said.

"When's that gonna be?" Cody asked, holding out a dripping plate for me to dry.

"Soon," I said. "Stop pestering me."

"No time like the present," Cody said, nodding out the window. "Here he comes. Dry off your hands, put on a smile, and tell him what's going on. You owe him the truth, Shelby. You need to tell him tonight."

"You're right," I said, drying my hands on a dish towel. "You got this?"

"Who do you think did the dishes while you were at school?" Cody said with a grin. He glanced out the window. Luke and Daddy were almost to the porch. "Go on. Tell him now."

* * *

"Sure is a nice night," Luke said as we walked hand in hand past the barn where we'd first made love. I resisted the urge to drag him inside and rip his clothes off. We hadn't made love since he'd been home and even though he put on a brave face, I knew his side still hurt him something fierce. The scar was healing up, but one good romp in the barn could send him back to the hospital. I wanted to fuck his brains out, but not at the cost of popping his stitches again.

We walked past the barn where the pastures started. About thirty yards out, at the top of a hill, was a giant elm tree that we used to climb when we were kids. It loomed dark and large as the sky behind it turned purple.

"Can you make it to the tree?" I asked, squeezing his hand.

"I think I can," he said, giving me a sideways smile.

I looked up at the stars that were starting to come out as we walked through the tall grass, trying to find the right words to tell Luke about the job. I had already played the conversation over and over in my mind, but I knew reality rarely mirrored imagination.

Did I really expect Luke to just forget about bull riding and move to Houston with me?

Did I really expect him to never climb onto the back of another bull at all?

Did I expect anything of him other than great sex?

Did I expect anything at all?

We reached the tree and Luke turned to sit on the ground.

"Need help?" I asked, holding Luke's hand as he lowered himself slowly to the ground.

"No, ma'am," he said, wincing. "I am quite capable of sitting down on my own. Though getting up might be another matter." He sat down and leaned back against the tree with his long legs stretched out and ankles crossed.

I sat down beside him and leaned my head on his shoulder. This was the closest we'd been in days without someone watching us. Immediately, I could feel the heat growing between my legs. I could feel my nipples pushing against the thick padding of my bra. I wanted him so bad I could already feel him inside me, but I knew we had to be careful. His stitches were still mending. And Daddy could show up anytime.

"This is nice," Luke said, brushing his lips against my forehead. "You wanna fool around?"

"Do you think we can without putting you back in the hospital," I said, putting my hand to his cheek and brushing my lips to his. I glanced toward the house at the bottom of the hill. I could see the lights on in the kitchen and front rooms. Where we were, under the night shade of the old elm, I was pretty certain that we couldn't be seen.

My hand slid over his thigh, just an inch or two away from his cock, which if past experience held true, was already growing hard and thick inside his jeans. I put my lips to his ear and swirled my tongue around the rim.

"So, what are you plans?" Luke asked of out of the blue. My hand froze on his thigh as I pulled back to look him in the eye.

"Plans? What do you mean?" I held my breath, wondering if he had somehow found out about my job. I pulled my hand back from his leg and laced my fingers together in my lap.

"I mean, you know, do you plan on staying here on the ranch or maybe getting a job somewhere else? I'm not sure where a body has to move to work on seeds."

"Well, I haven't given it much thought," I said, lying through my teeth because I wasn't prepared to tell him the truth. I glanced at him sideways. "What about you? What are your plans?"

Luke stared off toward the house. He brought up his knees and rested his elbows on them. I could just make out his profile in the darkness. He said, "Reckon I'll get back on the circuit someday."

I frowned at him. "Is that for sure what you're gonna do?"

His shoulder went up and down against mine. "Don't really know," he said quietly. "Reckon I won't make any firm plans until I know that I'm well enough to ride again."

"That's smart," I said, wrapping my arms around myself as if I were chilly. I wasn't. I just didn't know what to do with my hands.

"I can't imagine you'd stick around here," he said. "You have your degree now. I'm sure there's a bunch of companies that would love to scoop you up."

"Well, I'm not sure about that," I said. My stomach started to sour. I could taste the bitter hint of bile in my throat. I hated lying to him. It was twisting me into knots. I took a deep breath and decided to tell him the truth. It had to come out sooner or later. Now was as good a time as any.

Then I felt his hand on my leg.

"What are you doing?" I asked, smiling, suddenly breathing hard in response to his touch. He turned toward me with his hand sliding into my crotch. My pussy was scorching hot for him. I could feel the juices pooling in the crotch of my cotton panties. He squeezed my pussy and my juices soaked into my jeans. I spread my legs and sighed.

"We can talk plans later," he said, his lips on mine. He swirled his tongue around my lips, then pushed his tongue into my mouth. "Right now, I gotta have you or I'm gonna bust right out of these jeans.

"Stop, let me do the hard work," I said. I glanced toward the house again. I could see Daddy through the window of his study, smoking his pipe and reading a book. I didn't see Cody, but figured he was smart enough not to have followed us out to the tree.

Under cover of darkness, I pulled off my boots and shimmied out of my jeans and helped Luke shimmy out of his. He lay back against the tree with his rock-hard cock in his hand, stroking it slowly, waiting for me to climb onboard.

"If your side starts to hurt we'll stop," I said, turning my ass toward him and slowly squatting to lower my pussy onto his waiting cock. The breath caught in my throat when the head of his cock slid inside me. I squatted down a little more and more of him slid inside me. When he was in as far as he could go, I began to rock my hips back and forth, milking him slowly, like sliding over a saddle on a slow trotting horse.

"Fuck..." Luke moaned. "Now that's the best medicine there is."

He slid his hands under my ass to help take some of the weight off my knees. He dug his fingers into my ass and helped me rock back and forth. I moaned as the length of him slid in and out of my soaking cunt. I was gushing, dripping, covering his cock and balls with my juices. My tangy scent wafted through the moist night air.

"Jesus... Luke... I'm cumming... already..." I sighed, squeezing my eyes shut as his thick cock slid in and out. I brought my hands to my tits and gave them a firm squeeze. My rigid nipples pushed out from my bra and t-shirt. I rolled my fingers over them as the heat of my orgasm started to burn its way throughout my body.

"Shit... Shelby... cum... baby..." Luke said, panting the words, fingers flexing on my ass. "I'm... right behind you..."

I bit my lip to keep from screaming as the orgasm shot through me like lightning in a Texas thunderstorm, making me shudder as my body released wave after wave of slick cum down the length of his cock and balls.

Luke came with me, clenching his hands on my ass and pulling me down onto him as far as I could go. I heard him grunt like a bear as the heat of his hot milky orgasm filled my cunt. I could feel his heat burning from my clit to my nipples. His hard thrusts pushed the air from my lungs.

I braced my hands on my knees and struggled to catch my breath. I could hear Luke panting like a dog behind me. His fingers loosened on my ass. He started gently massaging the small of my back with his thumbs.

"Jesus Christ a'mighty, I needed that," Luke said with a happy sigh.

"So did I," I said, pushing myself up off him with a grunt. I turned around to squat over his deflated cock again, this time facing him. I put my hands around his neck and pressed my lips to his. "Your side okay?"

"Yes, ma'am, my side's just fine.

"What were we talking about?" I asked, nuzzling my nose to his.

"Damned if I can remember," he said as his tongue pushed into my mouth again. "Damned if I can remember."

Luke

After a week back home at the ranch, I was feeling more like my old self. I wasn't quite ready to climb back on a bull, but I had high hopes that someday I would.

Shelby turned out to be one hell of a nurse, although she could be a Nazi at times. We hadn't managed to sneak off and have sex again after our night under the old tree, but she was sweet and attentive and waited on me hand and foot. It was kinda nice.

Course, it would have been nicer to take her out to the barn and let her ride my old pecker like a show pony. But that time would come. Right now, she seemed to have other things on her mind.

I could tell something was eating at her by the way she got quiet when I talked about getting back on the circuit and maybe taking her with me. She wouldn't say yes or no when I asked her if she might come along. She'd just look me in the eye and say, "We'll see."

Then, Friday night, when I'd been home a week, we were sitting on the front porch swing after dinner watching the sun go down when she said she had something to tell me.

She had gotten a job, she said, one she'd applied for when she was still in grad school months ago.

It was her dream job, messing with seeds or something like that.

She had to be in Houston by Sunday night to start on Monday morning.

The company had rented her a place to stay, a furnished apartment downtown. She could live there rent-free for three months to give her time to find a permanent place.

I couldn't recall ever seeing her so excited

She wanted me to come with her.

She was gonna make lots of money and could support us both.

What did I think?

Didn't that sound great?

"Well, I don't know what to think," I said honestly. "I mean, this is kind of out of the blue."

"Yes, well, I mean I know it is," she said. Our legs were pressed together on the swing. My hand was on my knee. She reached over and covered it with her hand. "But think of it as an opportunity."

"An opportunity to do what?" I asked.

"Well, to get off the circuit for good," she said, squeezing my hand. "An opportunity to do something real with your life."

I frowned at her. "I have done something real with my life," I said.

"Well, I know, but I'm talking about doing something meaningful."

I kept frowning at her. If this was her way of delivering "good news" she wasn't very good at it.

I snapped a little at her. "Something meaningful, like working on seeds."

She took her hand off mine. "Well, yes, something other than riding silly old bulls."

I huffed at her. "Shelby, I have ridden a lot of bulls, but never one that was silly or old."

"You know what I mean," she said.

I shook my head. "No, ma'am, I don't think I know what you mean. How about you explain it to me?"

She turned sideways in the swing to face me. "Luke, how long do you think you can ride bulls for a living?"

"I don't ride bulls for a living," I said honestly. "Hell, they're ain't much of a living in it."

"Exactly, so why do you do it?" She let her pretty eyes go around my face, like she was searching for the answer. "I mean, you've done it for six years and the only thing you have to show for it is a body covered with scars and a couple of silly belt buckles."

"Silly belt buckles," I said. I was starting to seethe. I hadn't been mad at anybody in a long time. I try to keep an even temper because I tend to do and say things I regret when I get mad. I dug my fingers into my knees and took a deep breath.

"Are you all right?" she asked. "Your face is getting awfully red."

"Shelby, have you ever seen me mad?" I asked.

She thought about it for a moment. "No, I don't reckon I have."

I turned to glare at her. "Well, this is what mad looks like on me."

She swallowed hard. "Well, I don't think I like it."

"Well, I'm sorry, but you brought it on," I said, throwing my hands in the air. "Tell a man that he's wasted his life doing meaningless things and this is what you get, Lil Sis." I shook my head and tried to lower my boiling point a little. I didn't want to go off on her, but goddamn it all, she was basically saying that I had wasted my life chasing a dream that didn't mean jack shit. And now she wanted me to move to Houston and do what, keep house for her? No fucking way!

Before I could say anything more, she put a hand on my arm and gave it a squeeze. "Oh my lord, do you know what this is?"

I was still seething. I stared at the horizon and said, "A bunch of shit?"

"No, it's déjà vu."

That made me glance her way. "Deja what?"

"Déjà vu," she said with a soft smile. "It's when you get that feeling that you've already experienced something before."

"You mean like us sitting here on this swing while you telling me how I've wasted my life."

"Something like that," she said, her fingers digging into my arm and giving it a shake so I'd look at her. "We had a similar conversation right here six years ago, when I was trying to get you to move to College Station with me."

She was right. I remembered. I smiled and shook my head. "I'll be damned," I said. "You're right." I stared into her eyes and put my hand on top of hers. "As I recall, that conversation didn't end well. And we didn't speak for six years."

"Because I was a stupid girl," she said. Her eyes welled with tears. She cupped my chin with her free hand. "I thought my dreams were more important than yours. I wanted you to forget about what you wanted and just come with me." She bit her bottom lip as a tear streamed down her cheek. "And I'm doing it again."

I felt every ounce of anger leave my body as I put my hand on her cheek. "Shelby, I'm so proud for you. I know this is your dream job. I'm thrilled that your dreams are coming true. But you have to understand, I have dreams, too. They may not be as lofty as yours or pay anywhere as much, and usually I end up on my ass in the dirt, but it's still my dream and I can't ignore it. Do you understand?"

"I do," she said, leaning her forehead to rest against mine. "I reckon we just have to figure out how we can both chase our dreams and not lose each other again."

"Think we can?" I asked.

"Yes," she said, kissing me even though her Daddy and Cody were milling around inside the house. "I think we can."

EPILOG: Shelby

I left for Houston that Sunday night and started my new job on Monday morning. I was immediately in my element. They handed me a lab coat and showed me to the lab and my heart did a happy dance. It was hard to believe this little girl from a dusty Texas cattle ranch was now doing research and development to create hybrid seeds that would help feed the world.

The apartment they provided was nice: one bedroom, two baths, a decent sized kitchen. I couldn't cook for shit, so I was glad to discover that downtown Houston was packed with restaurants, from fast food to gourmet. I usually ended up somewhere in the middle, though Luke always wanted a big steak when he was in town and hungry for a meal. Sometimes, after a good ride, he would even pick up the tab. Insert smiley face here...

Luke mended at the ranch for another week after I left, then joined me in Houston until the fall rodeo season started. After a few weeks, he claimed that he was good as new and ready to ride. His ability to drive me over the moon in the bedroom had returned in full force, but I made him bring me a note from the doctor that officially said he could go back to riding bulls.

He called me a Nazi, but I didn't mind.

I would have hogtied that boy to the bed to keep him from getting back on a bull before his body was ready.

Hmmm...

Hogtie him to a bed, now that was a very interesting idea...

* * *

My intention was to hogtie Luke to the bed, but he said only if I went first. So, there I was, naked as a jaybird, spread eagle on the bed, with my wrists and ankles tied with scarves to the corner posts.

Luke climbed onto the bed and got to his knees between my legs. My pussy was already sopping wet. It had started flowing like a river the moment I laid down and he started tying me up. I bit my bottom lip and watched Luke take his long cock in his hand. He grinned at me as he stroked its full length, bringing it to maximum size in an instant.

The head was large and purple.

Just looking at it made my blood boil and my juices flow.

I wiggled my ass on the bed and gave him a nod.

"You gonna just play with that thing or stick it inside me?"

"Actually, I thought about going out for a beer," he said with an evil grin, his free hand now sliding between my legs, moving up and down across my wet folds. "I mean, since you're all tied up."

"Don't you dare," I said. "This was my idea. You can't turn it around on me."

"Don't worry," Luke said, moving closer so he could swish around the head of his cock against my glory hole. "I ain't going anywhere except here."

I closed my eyes as the head of his cock slid inside me, prying open my tight pussy. I pulled against the restraints, wanting to put my hands on him, but he had me tied tight.

"You ain't going anywhere either," he said, sliding in an inch, then another, then another. I felt the tip of his cock hit my cervix. I swallowed hard and closed my eyes.

Luke braced his hands on the bed beside me and starting moving his hips back and forth. I could feel him everywhere, as if he had invaded my body. My pussy tightened around his cock, gripping him, milking him as he slid in and out.

"God... Shelby..." he said, the words coming in gusts as he pumped in and out of me. "Damn... girl... your pussy... so fucking... tight..."

"Fuck me hard," I moaned, staring into his eyes. My nipples were like large pink thimbles. I ached to have him touch them.

As if he could read my mind, Luke's hands found my tits and he squeezed my nipples hard between his fingers, sending shockwaves of pain and pleasure shuddering through me.

Luke's hips started moving faster, thrusting into me, making the headboard slam into the wall. My tits flounced in his hands. His cock slid over my clit as he jackhammered into me. I could feel the orgasm building in me, like a raging flood about to burst through a dam.

"Fuck... Luke... I'm... cumming..."

He hammered faster. I could feel him in my chest, my throat, my head. "I'm ... cumming... too..."

The bed literally shook as he rammed his huge cock in and out of my slippery cunt. I thought we were going to knock the pictures off the wall. My orgasm shuddered through me and burst from my pussy, gushing hot tangy juice over Luke's entire cock and balls.

I felt Luke stiffen and his cock pulsated inside me, filling my cunt with his hot milky cum, warming me from the inside out. I blew out the breath I'd been holding and let my body go limp.

I opened my eyes to find him watching me with a smile on his face. He was moving his hips slowly, his cock still inside me, both of us a sticky mess.

"I think I'm having that déjà vu stuff," he said.

"The feeling that you've been here, done this before?" I asked with a dreamy smile.

"Yes, ma'am," he said, lowering his lips to mine. "I hope I have it till the day I die."

"Me, too," I sighed. "Many, many years from now."

THE END

Don't miss out!

Visit the website below and you can sign up to receive emails whenever Amy Brent publishes a new book. There's no charge and no obligation.

https://books2read.com/r/B-A-GACH-UIPMB

BOOKS 2 READ

Connecting independent readers to independent writers.

Did you love *Filthy Cowboy*? Then you should read *Filthy Coach*[1] by
Amy Brent!

**What do you do when the sexiest bastard to walk on to football
field happens to need your personal services?**

Sam Carson is a washed-up ex-quarterback who's more famous for
his drunken brawls and internet sex tapes than throwing touchdowns.
So why did my father, the owner of the Atlanta Trojans, hire Sam to be
the new head coach? And what part does he expect me to play in this
dangerous game?

ALLIE WINSTON: I'm a tough chick playing in a tough man's
game. I'm a sports image consultant. It's my job to make undisciplined
football players and unfriendly coaches heroes in the public eye. But
when I'm assigned to make Sam Carson look good, I know that I have

---

1. https://books2read.com/u/3n726P

2. https://books2read.com/u/3n726P

my work cut out for me. Especially when he catches me in the shower diddling myself and moaning his name. I can't deny my feelings for Sam, but I can't deny that I'm also part of a game that's using Sam as a pawn. I can only hope that he never discovers my treachery, because I can't imagine my life without Sam in my bed.

SAM CARSON: I'll be the first to admit it. I'm a baaaad boy. I drink hard, play hard, and screw hard. And when I drive my Lambo into the back of a truck, my career as one of the hottest quarterbacks in pro football comes to an end. For the last few years I've been a coach. When I get an offer to be the head coach of the Atlanta Trojans, I know something is fishy. Then I meet Allie Winston, the smoking hot daughter of the team owner. I want her and I know she wants me, but I get the feeling that there's more than just sexual attraction at play. Allie seems to be playing a dangerous game, and I won't stop until I find out exactly what – and who - is going down.

Also by Amy Brent

Filthy
Filthy Boss
Filthy Doctor
Filthy Professor
Filthy Seal
Filthy Cowboy
Filthy Daddy
Filthy Coach

Forbidded
The Doctor's Fake Marriage

Forbidden
Fake Fiance
One More Chance
Crave Me
My Best Friend's Dad
The Doctor's Fake Marriage
Dad's Best Friend

Forbidden Fantasies
Daddy's Business Partner
Daddy's Friend
Daddy O
Climbing His Corporate Ladder
Taken By Daddy's Boss
Filthy Liar

Standalone
Teachers' Pet
Filthy Box Set
Knocked Up By My Brother's Best Friend
My Best Friend's Brother
My Best Friend's Ex
Say You're Mine
Club Desire Box Set
My Boyfriend's Dad
Fighting For Her
Forbidden Love Box Set
Love Undercover
Friends With Benefits
A Royal Menage
Baby Fever
Vegas Baby
Brother's Best Friend for Christmas
Christmas With My Best Friend's Dad
My Son's Sitter
Single Dad's Christmas Present
Surrendering To 3 Alphas

Because I Love You
Catching Up With Daddy
Claiming Cinderella
Double Trouble
First Love
First Time
Knocked Up By My Brother's Best Friend
My Best Friend's Boyfriend
Pretend Daddy
Redemption
Roomies With Benefits
Royally Yours
Rub Me The Right Way
Show Stopper
That One Night
The Baby Contract
Truth Or Dare
Santa's Naughty List
Quickie on Christmas
Con Man

www.ingramcontent.com/pod-product-compliance
Lightning Source LLC
Chambersburg PA
CBHW050546160726
48003CB00002B/774